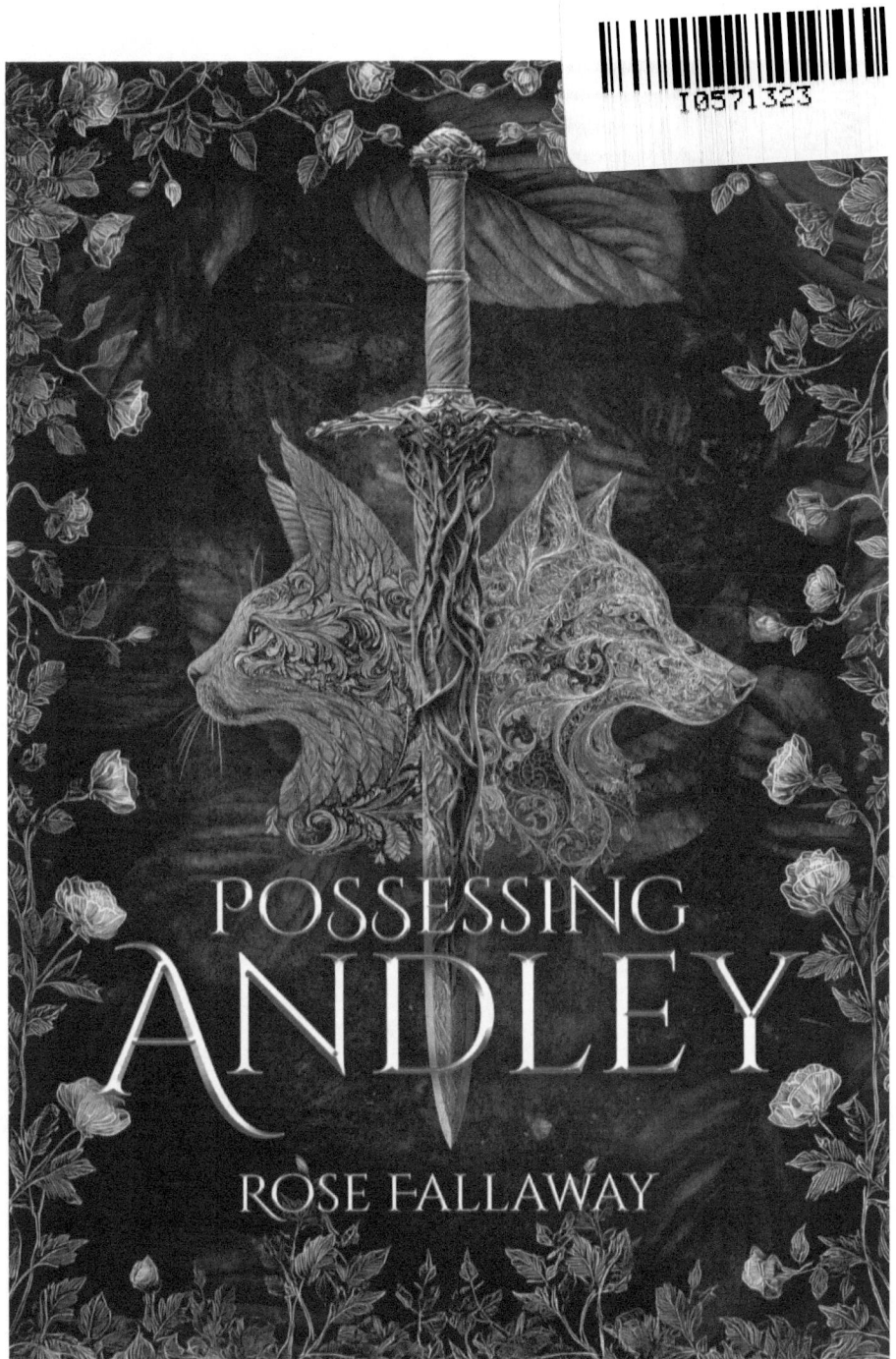

POSSESSING ANDLEY

ROSE FALLAWAY

Table of Contents

POSSESSING
ANDLEY

ROSE FALLAWAY

Possessing Andley

Copyright © 2025 Rose Fallaway

Editing, formatting and cover design by:

www.letsgetbooked.com

ISBN 978-1-0696728-1-0

Trigger warnings for:

Sexual assault

Domestic abuse

Mention of suicide

Chapter 1

Andley

A trail was worn into the grass-covered corridor by passaging nobles, vassals and soldiers serving from within the forest castle over innumerable generations. Yet, it never became wild. The careful tending of the keepers kept it from rot or decay. I walked barefoot between walls of birch trees arching high overhead, carefully ignoring the daunting thoughts pawing at the edges of my mind. Above, a ceiling of braided vines and branches swayed in the breeze outside, casting shimmering circles of light that danced like reflections on water.

"Dancing faeries ... Leadanah, do you remember?" I asked her in thought, sending the question inward to my therio. Leadanah stirred within our shared mind and stretch into wakefulness. As she did so, a memory from her childhood flooded into my consciousness.

"What are those lights on the ground, Mother?" Leadanah had asked.

"They are the faeries, Leadanah. Climb higher, shake the canopy, and make them dance."

Leadanah had already been too old to believe in faeries, but if Mother had said the water held the moon, or that light was faeries, then she would make it true. Just to see her smile.

Small, clawed hands grasped at thin branches, shoving aside the leaves until Leadanah reached the top. There, she held the branches stretching overhead and swung her body down to dangle from the ceiling of entwined tree branches and vines. Leadanah's small, feathered wings burst from between her shoulder blades, above the low draping robe lining her back.

She fluttered them wildly, rocking herself back and forth. The circles of light below bounced merrily as little leaves fluttered to the ground around Mother.

She looked up, beaming at the untamed little therio. Leadanah released the branch, and I watched the ground race up as she plopped down before Mother, for even she didn't know yet that she should fly. Leadanah held her arms up in a silent request to be held. Mother leaned down, scooping up the young therio and planted kisses on her soft furred cheeks. The sharp voice of Spildey, father's adviser, sheared through the happiness.

"Leadanah, bring Lady Andley back now. You have had enough time out today."

Leadanah's fur rose along her nape, and she let out a childish hiss from over mother's shoulder.

Mother whispered into her little ear. "You are not a wild animal, Leadanah. Do not make such sounds at others. We must sometimes obey when we do not want to. I will see you at bedtime."

Leadanah lifted her chin from Mother's shoulder and leaned back, glaring at her. She pressed her tiny, clawed hands against her mother's cheeks, squeezing them inward. I could sense the wretched anger within her recede as Mother locked her eyes with her. Leadanah pressed Mother's cheeks harder, making her lips purse outwards.

"Ducky face kisses!" she cried gleefully.

"Ducky kisses!" Mother echoed through her still-pursed lips.

Mother pulled Leadanah's face toward her and pressed her squished lips repeatedly all over her cheeks, forehead, and lips. Leadanah squealed, laughing, and pressed her kitten nose on Mother's face in return. Our mother pressed her forehead into Leadanah's, looking up at her from beneath long eyelashes, smiling with kindly finality. Leadanah returned her smile with a downward twitch in the corners of her mouth and a slight scrunching of her nose. She released her cheeks and sat up straight.

As the sight of Mother faded, Spildey's voice returned, commenting on how it was time for Andley to integrate her therio.

"Lady Andley's therio has far too much control. You had better nip it in the bud before she takes over completely."

Our body shifted from her therio form into my human form. Leadanah's fangs receded into blunted children's teeth and the hundreds of thin sharp quills covering her head fell back into my own loose colorless hair. The feathers covering Leadanah's torso melded back into soft skin while the fur covering her legs receded into her body. Her wings folded, pressing hard against my back. I could feel them being absorbed into my body as they finally dissolved away.

Anger and sadness rose in Leadanah as she cut herself off from me. That day had been happy. He often chastised Leadanah into retreat. She had been the one person who was not sorry when he later went missing. Leadanah never shared much of her pain with me, but I knew it was there, always lingering in everything good she had. I remembered that day as well, but I never associated the dancing lights with sadness. I had returned to control the body we shared and spent the rest of that day with Mother.

She'd kissed me goodnight at bedtime and asked to see Leadanah to kiss her, too. Mother and Father always treated us like we were separate people. I often still feel pain at their loss, but sometimes, when Leadanah thinks of them and the feeling slips through from her, it is so immense that mine seems a drop of water in a raging river in comparison.

I reached the entrance of my private rooms before I was ready. Taking a shuddering breath, I entered the chamber to face the magistrate from Sandor.

Last year we were blindsided by the sudden aggression of Brath, the kingdom in the mountains south of us, which lies on the other side of the valley. They had long been a trading partner to us and took no part for or against our fight with Sandor to become an independent kingdom. They have, without discernible reason, blocked our access to the valley which the two countries have shared peacefully as common land between us for generations.

A shrill voice startled me, invading the silence as I entered my chambers. "Which form will you prefer during the consummation ceremony?"

The magistrate stood on fragile deer-like hind quarters, his back ridged in his immaculately arranged suit. I found myself suddenly offended to see him standing there in his therio form, a signal of aggression or authority

9

when presented among strangers or masters. He looked down his elongated nose at me, waiting for my response.

"Ugh, wh-what?" I sputtered.

"Your preferred form, dear, for the consummation. Prince Marston will allow your preference for a portion of the ceremony. Which is it?" He spoke with dry irritation.

"Oh, I, I'd really rather not," I said, staring at my feet. A cold trickle of dread poured down my back.

"I don't want … my guardian said he'd request that the consummation is skipped," I said.

"He did, sweety. Price Marston has denied the request but has graciously agreed to allow your preferred form for a portion of the ceremony, as I have already said. To help you get comfortable." He tried to sound sympathetic, but his tone came out practiced and hollow.

"Only human. Please. Will he please agree to just our human forms?"

"Oh, a shame, your mate is quite looking forward to experiencing your therio."

A rush of blood reddened my cheeks, accompanied by a threat of hot tears. I envisioned Leadanah's clawed hands reaching out from the darkness, bending back the Prince's ringed fingers as they wandered over her.

"I was told you are shy with your therio. I shall, ugh, inquire," he said, this time his pity seemed genuine.

"I, I won't use my therio form. Inform him."

"Right. I'll um, inform him," he said.

The magistrate cocked an eyebrow at me before he turned away sharply, nearly whipping me with his bony tail. He stalked off on stiff hind quarters through the arched oak roots that made up the entrance to my private den.

I realized that in my anxiety I'd been breathing in more than out. I released the stale air out of my lungs, slumping my shoulders as the newly empty space in my chest made room for my heart to finally sink.

My hand maid was gazing at me with her mouth hanging open, dumbfounded. Her usual mild human form had slipped slightly, so she took on her dimidium form, causing her to appear half human and half of her fox-type therio. A sure sign of mindless distraction.

"Marlette, please pick a form," I said as I dropped into the chair before my vanity.

"Right, my lady, I didn't mean to offend. Of course." She was silent for a moment as she worked to compose herself. The red fur lining her cheekbones retracted slowly, and she laid her pointed ears down to be reabsorbed back into her deep auburn hair. I watched her intently, a little sad, but also fascinated to know there was no other person within her and that she controlled her therio form and human form equally. She, like all others, had undergone integration as expected. I remembered her therio though, that second person within her, it had called itself Yidya. Mostly, Yidya had yipped and barked and was easy to please. Much more like a pet than a person.

"My lady, don't you think your therio is most appropriate for the occasion? I mean, your rarity alone. It would be such a … a beautiful ceremony. The Prince is also very majestic. My lady, as rumor has it. I think it … is expected …" she trailed off apologetically.

My face flushed once again with both anger and embarrassment. I picked up my hairbrush as calmly as my shaking hands would allow.

"Oh my lady, my apologies. I will do it." She rushed forward and grabbed hastily at the gold crested brush in my hands.

"No, Marlette. Leave," I snapped, stopping myself as I saw her stricken face. "I am sorry, I just want to be alone," I finished.

I bowed my head low to expose the back of my neck, requesting her pardon. Marlette tapped my nape lightly, curtsied, and hustled out the same way the magistrate did, pulling the black glittering curtain. Her little sob lingered in the room with me as she padded away.

God, I just hate all of them, I thought with exhausted anger.

A deep feminine voice echoed through my mind and reverberated through me like a gravelly purr.

"Andley, what is all this? Why do I hear your thoughts cutting through the peace and quiet?"

"Because I am surrounded by enemies on one side and fools on the other. He wants the consummation ceremony. He wants you!" I said all this inwardly, so only Leadanah could hear as I shared the memory of my conversation with the Prince's magistrate with her. There was a long silence. I thought she had receded to leave me alone with these worries.

"He may not," Leadanah finally replied.

"No, he may not. You are not for having or giving," I agreed.

"I will kill him. Does he also wish to use his therio?" she mused. It would be like fucking a Gollum, no doubt. The way they call up the bodies of the dead within them.

"I hear he is very proud of his therio, and he only uses it in the presence of others for great showing and power displays," I thought back to her.

Leadanah scoffed. "I will *display* his guts if he tries to wield power over me."

"Leadanah, don't you understand? This is serious. You can't kill him. You can't do anything to him. I hear he's huge. He is a prince. He can take the whole pack and do what he wants with us. Right now, we have a bigger problem than the consummation ceremony."

My mind conjured up an image of a bed lit as though the sun itself stared down at it, my naked body laying limp beneath the bulk of a cruel man. All the while faceless strangers oooh and ahhhed with every humiliating thrust. The public consummation of a royal marriage held deep roots in both Brath and the forest, but never have they occurred without the consent of the bride's guardian. Rathon did not consent. This should have been the end of it.

Leadanah chuckled, ignoring my fear.

"He cannot kill Rathon's whole pack. If they could do that, you'd have lost the rebellion against Brath and you'd not be in this mess."

"The ceremony is a problem, yes, but the real problem is how are we going to keep hiding ourselves? We should have integrated long ago. I don't know if we can hide it after this," I thought.

"Andley, I told you before, if you even think of integrating me, I will tear your mind to pieces and take over this body. You will not integrate me," she hissed into my mind.

From what I had been told as a child, the human mind absorbs the therio's mind upon integration. The two minds form into one. Because a therio's mind is not fully developed and is typically only partially self-aware creature, the human mind only alters as it takes in the therio's consciousness. Some become tougher and more aggressive, and some develop a fearful timidness depending on the disposition of their therio. After this, they can control their body to shift into their human form or the animal like therio form without the therio consciousness being there. Typically, a therio's mind is not as fully conscious and self aware as Leadanah. When it happens, they integrate the therio before it overpowers the human mind. It is exceedingly rare that a therio's mind is given the opportunity to take over the human and in cases such as this it does seem that the human mind is destroyed. The therio doesn't take on any traits from the human mind. We call these therio who have destroyed the human mind within rogues, or wild ones. I was still unsure if Leadanah could take over, but more importantly I knew she never would, regardless.

"Calm down, I don't want to. I like you where you are and I like myself as I am. It's everyone else who doesn't want me."

"They don't really want me either, Andley. They want the idea of me. Only the rogue ones know me and even they don't really want me," Leadanah said. "Come on, let's not think about this right now."

A quick succession of images flashed through my mind as Leadanah thought of her rogue lover and the pleasures she found with him, there in the unknowable darkness. I gasped in surprise as heat crept down my lower abdomen. I squirmed as the images receded.

"Leadanah, you saw him again and didn't wake me? I complained. Leadanah let out a low chuckle inside our body and let a few more little flashes come through.

"Does it bother you?" she teased.

She pushed through, beginning to take over.

"Leadanah, stop that. This is serious," I said, but did not resist her.

My face slid into Leadanah's short feline snout, white velvety fur replaced the skin to the edges of my cheekbones. I watched my lips part, splitting into a devilish grin and expose sharp pointed teeth. Leadanah opened what was now her mouth, and laughed with her usual mischievous mirth, my words unheeded.

"It is sooo serious," she taunted in a false pout. "I will show you all I did last night while you were asleep."

She let through another images: clawed hands on a muscular chest, digging into skin. Her wings falling forward into the corner of my view, the sharp finger like appendages on their tips digging into the soil like gnarled tree roots. Their bodies rocking feverishly. I heard the rapid, short breath of the rogue one laying on the forest floor between Leadanah's muscular thighs.

"You never take anything seriously." I sighed, yet I felt delighted.

Our minds and body balanced comfortably into our dimidium, the form where the body became a blend of the therio and human. This is the most natural state for all people. For others, because there was a single human mind that controlled both the therio form and the human form, being in dimidium was simply a state of relaxation, like relaxing a flexed muscle. But for Leadanah and I, being in dimidium meant something else altogether. It was as near to being a single entity as we could become.

While the body was balanced equally between my human form and her therio form, our minds could merge to some extent. We each perceived only what the other willingly shared. It was the only state where I could physically see what her therio form might look like, although only partially formed. In dimidium, my face remained mostly the same, although my teeth became sharp and slightly elongated, and my nose became a short snout. Leadanah's wings came out, and were covered in short blue feathers on the back. My torso would sprout soft white feathers, and white fur grew along my legs. In this state, both of our consciousness were equally present.

Our dimidium form wasn't one we took on often, as it could sometimes be awkward to move our body like this. The blended part of our minds could perceive and react reflexively to what movement we both wanted to make. But if I had an idea go to one way and Leadanah wanted to go another, this resulted in a sort of intense painful flexing of the body, resulting in no movement at all.

Usually, we only took on our dimidium form if we wanted to feel closer to each other, or to share something the other was seeing or feeling more closely. We didn't have to be in dimidium to exchange memories with each other, but it made them more visceral, like we could really feel what the other felt during the memory. Such as the memory of being touched or the way something tasted.

I took in the memory of the night she'd shared with the rogue. The subtle sense of lust and violence which always accompanied Leadanah crept upon me, and we rose, walking to the canopy bed. Leadanah and I giggled mischievously together as her memories poured into me. We threw ourself backward onto the bed landing on our wings and cradling ourselves in them. The talons extended from our pawed feet as we drew our hands up and plunged them downwards between our thighs. The last coherent thought I had as myself was admiring the blue green bioluminescent glow worms winding deep throughout the crevassed ceiling of the thick oak roots stretching overhead.

Chapter 2

Leadanah

While Andley faded into sleep, I lay awake, gaining full consciousness slowly, creeping into the body that Andley and I shared, inch by inch as it slowly morphed into my form. Andley's fingers stretched into the clawed talons of my own hands. The silver white flesh of my wings thickened. A slow burning sensation laced its way along the back of my wings, rolling down back and shoulders as strong midnight-blue feathers layered over me, meeting the fur encompassing my hips.

I flexed the sharp finger-like claws at my wingtips as they unfurled beneath me, stretching to their full span as I rolled over onto my stomach. As the feathers spread, they became short and soft, shifting from the deep blue along my back to a paler shade over my shoulders and arms, eventually fading to white as they covered my breasts and torso. Andley's legs lengthened, widening with my own powerful muscles. Soft white fur covered me from my hips to my feet, which became something between wolf paws and the talons of a predatory bird.

The soft length of Andley's hair became ridged from the root downward. The strands pulled themselves together as though they were living ropes, forming into locks of sharp, colorless quills covering my head. They created a stiff, nearly translucent curtain down my back. I rose from the bed, lowering my wings to wrap them comfortably around my waist like a skirt. I strode to the mirror and admired myself, appreciating the way my catlike nose twitched, and the black pools of my eyes caught the blue light emanating from the glow worms working their way through the roots of the den Andley and I shared. I smoothed the short fur along my face and smiled at myself, exposing a row of sharp teeth.

A scene from Andley's troubled dream floated into my consciousness momentarily. Rathon passed her to a hulking, faceless man, his claws outstretched, clutching at her breast. I shut the image out and closed the wall between her mind and my own. We could still flee, I mused. It wasn't too late. I sniffed. I had suggested this on several occasions; she refused each time. What good could this idiotic treaty do them? All that would result is Andley and I would be slaves to Prince Marston. Sandro would never come to Rathon's aid. Give their troops over? Ridiculous. Surely, they wouldn't fight for any kingdom but their own. Why any soldier even does that is beyond my understanding. Even if Sandor kept its word, Andley would be nothing more than a pawn to take power in the forest and overthrow Rathon. He's not a stupid man, so why did he think this would work? Why not simply send his wolves into Brath and kill their king? Wouldn't that end their war of attrition?

I slipped through the curtained doorway into the long corridor. The only light within was that of the moon entering through gaps in the branches overhead and the shimmer of lightning bugs blinking in and out like spirit orbs. There were no torches in this section of the castle. The walls grew too close together to allow for open flames. As I passed from the maze of corridors leading into the dens of the Castle nobles, I hid myself in the shadows swaying within the wall of trees until I reached the archway to the main hall. There was a sound of rustling leaves as the scent of freshly cut leaves and branches wafted onto my path. One of the keepers; they were always nocturnal types. I considered taking the servants' corridor out, but I did not feel like going backward and all the way around just to avoid one servant. I pressed forward into the hall, cutting a path along the tree line.

"Lady Andley?"

I froze.

"My lady, can you not sleep?"

I recognized the wisp-like figure crouched down on the far side of the hall with her back to me. While she waited for me to respond, Dalya

17

continued her steadfast work, weaving shoots of new growth in the trees together, tightening the wall inch by inch.

"No, miss Dalya, I cannot sleep tonight. I thought a walk would help."

"Nervous no doubt. An awful business, this is. Terrible."

She clicked her lips together, making a disparaging tutting sound at this. With her back to me, hands weaving continuously, as she spun her head around to face me. Her giant round, yellow eyes sought me out in the darkness, landing on my slinking form along the wall. It was like trying to conceal mountain.

"Why do you creep there, lady?"

"I didn't think you'd be here, I thought to sneak by." I smiled wryly at her. "Had I known, I'd have gone around the long way."

As clearly as Dalya could see me, I could also perceive her. I never asked her how her ancient eyes viewed things. If they saw in color or heat signature. Perhaps her night vision was a bright gray scale like mine. Dalya came from an old lineage of keepers, prehistoric and nearly extinct. Her therio species was as much reptilian as avian. Her kind was surprisingly docile for creatures that were clearly predatory.

"Perhaps you would have made it if I were not me. But you do not creep about in your own castle. Come out, Lady Andley. Take your walk. I'll not impede you."

Suddenly aware of how silly I looked, I stood to my full height. If I raised my arm, I could grab onto the ceiling branches. The people here had lived alongside Andley for twenty-four years, yet had such little awareness of her they mistook us for each other. When they saw me, which was exceedingly rare, they assumed Andley was simply in her therio form. It struck me as ridiculous. Even people in their therio forms act, move and speak the same as in their human form. For of course, there is only one person within them. How was it possible that they could not see the changes in Andley that were so pronounced, so obvious, for I did nothing to deceive them. They did not question it or even frown with doubt in my presence. What bothered me most was to know this and tell Andley, yet she still refused to abandon her duty to them.

As I left the confines of the castle, the spread of birch trees shifted into their natural state, no longer forced to grow and bend to the will of the keepers. They lined the shallow brooks descending from the hills into the valley river. As I passed the section of willow trees and entered the dense totems of ancient oak trees, I broke into a sprint, dodging them as they rushed upon me. My talons dug into the earth, etching long wounds into the damp soil in my wake.

The air of the forest, thick with humidity, coated my lungs, filling me with the essence of decaying leaves and the spice of oak bark. I moved through the last line of bowing trees into the clearing where the cart track leading to Sandor was cut and without stopping leaped into the air. My wings unfurled with equal swiftness, gave a single mighty beat, and I was abreast with the canopy.

I flew over the forest toward the valley, seeking signs of therios gathering, thinking amusedly about the rumours Andley's leaving must have generated. The wild therios had been surprisingly interested in the treaty with Sandor and the war with Brath.

Some tracks became apparent as I scanned the earth below. Soon the single path became many, converging together where the earth dipped into a large bowl. They must have been camped here together for a while, for there was a buildup of grass nests and shallow burrows.

Wild therios were typically solitary, having only one or two companions consistently. Even so, they often travel miles apart, only meeting up every few days. They gather in these clumps sporadically a few times a year to engage in trade, share news, tell stories, and fight, or fuck. As I circled the encampment of hide tents and pull carts and caravans, I found the familiar shape of Dante, galloping with a small fox-like child on his back. His red mane growing from his head flowed between his chiseled shoulders and along his spine and whipped wildly in the wind. I smiled, genuinely pleased to see him. I swooped down over his head and landed at a polite distance in front of him.

He slowed to a playful prance. The child had not noticed me yet and continued to laugh, bouncing gleefully on Dante's back, his little fists buried in his mane, holding on for dear life. Dante smiled at me after a short jolt of surprise upon seeing me before him. He reached over his head with both arms and grasped the little boy with his large hands, lifting him up and bringing him forward so the boy faced Dante upside down. The boy was still laughing and shouting curse words with the trusting joy of a boy with his favorite uncle.

Dante's voice was soft and deep when he spoke. "Lad, don't be frightened now. My friend Leadanah is here. If you scream, you'll offend her."

I raised an eyebrow. Not since I was a teenager have I been upset by the screams and gasps of others when they saw me. I crossed my arms and rested my wings about my waist, waiting for Dante to put the boy down. He flipped the boy upright and set him on his feet. The boy faced me. His upper lip twitched into a slight snarl, exposing one sharp canine tooth, and his eyes widened. I returned the snarl with a wry smile, showing him my teeth. The boy seemed to regain himself and instead of turning to run, he smiled brightly. I was surprised when he knocked a foot forward, heel ground firmly with his toes pointed into the air. He bents the knee of his other leg and leaned forward. The boy bowed low, looking up at me over his eyebrows.

"My lady." His boyish voice was a giggle. Then he stood up suddenly, eyes closed, his mouth open, and let out several yips of laughter and sprung away his red bushy tail bouncing steadily behind him.

"Bye Dante," he shouted.

Dante moved to my side, laughing as we watched the boy pounce on another child, rolling them both into the dirt.

"Little scamp. His father was noble in Brath. His mother tries to remind him to be polite. Mostly, their efforts result in playful mockery."

"Well, he didn't scream." I shrugged. "Why are therios from Brath here?"

"The conflict in the valley has pushed their migration north. They can't access their traditional hunting grounds."

I scowled at Dante as we walked shoulder to shoulder toward the center of the caravan.

"The treaty with Sandor may relive them?" I asked.

20

"Doubtful. If there's more fighting, the tribes will be in the middle. Some of them want to fight."

I scoffed. "Fight who?"

Dante looked incredulous. "King Rathon."

"Oh please, they aren't going to fight Rathon's wolves. Why not fight against Brath?

"Some think Brath should win."

I wasn't surprised to hear this. In the years since the rebellion, discontent with Rathon's rule throughout the wild therio tribes had steadily grown. The liberation from Sandor's oppressive governance had not freed the tribes like they'd hoped it would. While Rathon had banned the open kill law, allowing the murder of wild therios on sight, he had done nothing to include them into his new kingdom. He banned any permanent settlement of the tribes within the tree lines of his kingdom and banished wild therios from entering the forest townships, a breach which was still punishable with death.

"Brath does nothing for wild therios either. Why should the tribes care which country rules anywhere when we are subjects to none of them?"

"Some think we should be subjects. Some think Brath may grant us rights if we fight with them," Dante said.

"Wild therios would not make good citizens anywhere. We're more akin to animals. Why do they even want this?"

"Leadanah, while it's true that we are barely human, we're not animals."

"The tribes are angry they cannot go onto the villages like it's a right they have lost. But they never had that right t begin with. Do they forget the reasons we are not welcome? We're violent. We kill for fun as much as we kill for food. We kill each other, we kill villagers, we kill livestock." I was laughing at this, but the look on Dante's face gave me pause.

"We aren't all murderers or mad."

"I'm just saying, why do they want to be subjects when they are free now?"

"Come with me to the gathering. Listen to the leaders speak." Dante's usual slow, thoughtful cadence quickened, and his eyes gleamed as he spoke.

"There are many who think as you do, but they are trying to unite us. They believe they can negotiate with Brath for land rights in the valley."

"Dante, I did not seek you out so you could drag me to a meeting and listen to the hapless drivel of idiots. I don't care what the tribes are doing. I don't care about Brath or the Forest or Sandor. I am subject to none."

"Why have you come, then? Just lonely in all your freedom?" His voice held a hint of a growl.

"I came to see you."

I swung myself in front of him, blocking his path. Looking into his brown eyes, I ran one long talon down his hipbone to the line of short fur where his manhood lay sheathed beneath a rawhide cloth.

"Come to the meeting. We can go somewhere after." He grinned.

"No."

I smiled back at him, reaching beneath the cloth. My hand stroked the soft fur covering his cock, and it stiffened outward, beginning to emerge from beneath it. His lip twitched as he worked to control his desire. He grabbed my hand, pulling it aside.

"These are important meetings."

I ran my hands along his chest and leaned into him, my face tilted up to find his lips with my own.

"I won't come back later. It may be a long time before you have another chance to fuck me."

He let out a deep breath and pulled my hips into his, pressing me against his cock, which was now hanging low under the rawhide.

A fearful voice suddenly screamed out behind us. "Dante! Come quick we need help!"

We spun to face the crier. A reptilian woman was scampering along the ground on four limbs. She halted a foot in front of us and stood up, resting her weight on her muscular tail. She grasped Dante's tattooed forearm, tugging him forward.

"What's happened?" asked Dante.

"It's Justin. He's gone mad!"

22

The woman dropped back down. Turning away, she started back in the direction from which she'd come.

"Hurry! He's already killed three men!"

Dante drew the sword from a sheath strapped alongside his body. I stepped aside as he broke into a full gallop, moving away from the dust his hooves kicked up. Deciding I wanted to see how Dante fought and what kind of therio could warrant such a response, I strode in the direction Dante had chased the reptilian woman.

As I moved away from the center of the encampment, the shouts and primal roaring smothered the laughter and merriment of the therios left behind, who had no idea anything was amiss beyond their own tents. turning the corner of a large caravan there was a gap in the crowd as people made space for the scene at the center to play out.

The three large therio men lay dead and torn apart in separate heaps. In the center of these corpses, two fox-like figures lay crumpled together near an overturned fire pit. The larger of them lay, as if protectively on top of the much smaller therio. Its tiny, clawed hand and red fluffy tail lay limp, poking out from beneath the other. The light of flames from the still-burning firewood danced merrily in the pooling blood around them.

"The boy, the boy!" a desperate voice screamed.

While Dante and three others surrounded the enraged male, some of the onlookers attempted to reach the two fox-therios, in the vague hope that the child could still be saved. One woman dropped on all fours, her black ears laid back, her tail held out stiff ready to break into the chaos of fighting that took up the whole square. As she broke from the safety of shadows, light refracted in her green eyes, fixated on the body of what, in another situation, might have been her prey.

One of the fighting males passed unseeing before her path. She darted to the side, avoiding his massive claws as they tore away the grass in a spray while he lunged at his foe. She reached the huddled bodies and rolled the dead fox off the child. Its body splashed indignantly into the pool of blood at its side.

She took the child's forearm into her mouth and dragged him backward toward the tents. At that moment, the tin pot of another fire pit, thrown by Justin to evade his attackers, careened into the woman, striking her in the side and casting hot embers upon her silken fur. She let the boy's arm go as she cried out in pain and shock. She quickly reclaimed him in her jaws and continued her desperate, quick strides backward.

"She needs help!" Someone called.

Then cries sounded from the edges of the clearing. Two more therios emerged fearfully from the depth of shadows moving cautiously toward her. The boy still had not stirred, blood poured from his body. I turned my attention to the fighting of the five titan therios.

Justin, the mad therio, found himself encircled by the others. He swung a large boulder over his head. Rearing back, he threw it several feet but missed the reptilian therio before him. His bare, muscular chest heaved. Blood poured in streams from beneath the shafts of three arrows protruding from his stomach and shoulder, each having less effect than a splinter in the haze of his insanity. He fell forward, the knuckles of his massive hands thumping into the ground; his arms bearing the weight of his body.

He lunged, roaring at Dante, who had moved forwards swinging his sword, attempting to sever any limb he could catch from Justin's body. Justin side stepped the attack and stood up upon his haunches, beating his chest wildly, plunging the arrows deeper into his wounds. A therio resembling a bear, only a little taller than the mad therio before him, dashed forwards throwing him backward, but not knocking him off his feet. The bear dug his teeth into the side of Justin's neck. Justin opened his jaws once again in a monster out roar, revealing fierce canines. He reached into the sides of the bear's mouth with his powerful fingers and pried the jaws open. His strength surprised me as he continued to pull upon the lower jaw, attempting to pull it clean from his skull. The bear reeled back, clutching his face as blood splashed down the front of his chest. Justin continued to lunge at the bear, his hands open to grasp him around his neck. Dante and the two others sprang forth, blocking the path as the bear stumbled away, holding his jaw in place.

"Cantel, Cantel!" The calls of other therios went out to the bear. "Come to us here. Cantel follow our voices!"

The other therios hiding in the darkness though unable to fight for their size moved forth into the clearing. I watched them hunched over, darting into the clearing and back out into the shadows, trying to guide Cantel to safety. As I watched the bear, I noticed still the creatures trying to save the boy, who had abandoned the open. The boulder lay nearby the prone body of the therio who had been dragging him. She moaned, languishing where she lay.

It seemed the courage to save the boy had skipped over the others. None left the edges to pull them away. I looked at the fight. Once more, a massive feline pounced on Justin from behind. The mane covering his head and shoulders fell forwards, covering both of their faces from sight. Dante and the reptilian attacked from the front and on his side. I strode into the clearing toward the writhing and screaming therio. I thought she was speaking, but I couldn't make out the words over the chaos. When I reached her, I saw her ribs were concave and wondered if she could heal before she died.

I bent to lift her from the dirt. The words in her screams came clearly to me.

"The boy! Get the boy!"

I paused, surprised at her tenacity.

"He's dead," I said flatly and pressed my hands beneath her, trying not to cause more injury to her ribs.

"He's alive!" She gasped. "Leave me, he's alive."

I looked to the fox cub as he lay unmoving, eyes slit open, his mouth open and tongue lolling onto the ground beneath his cheek. That he had not reverted to his human form either meant he'd already integrated it, or that they were both dead.

"He's dead," I insisted and lifted her, intent on springing into flight.

The fighting meanwhile raged on and moved closer to where I stood.

"Put me down," she labored, pushing at my chest.

Frustrated, I huffed and bent back down. If she wanted to die to save a dead body that was her choice. I placed her back on the ground and turned

25

to the boy. Cradling him carefully, I crouched down, spreading my wings, and leaped upwards just above the tents and caravans surrounding us. Looking down, I found the group of onlookers huddled along the edges of the clearing. I swooped toward them landing among them. Within the group, a woman sat on her knees wailing and yipping, rocking with her face held in her hands. She had the same red fur as the boy I held. Meanwhile, a male therio was being held down by several others. He growled and snapped at them, straining to break free.

"Leadanah!" a familiar voice shouted.

Larson, a small mousy therio, stepped toward me. His whiskers twitching madly as he reached out to the boy in my arms.

"You have him. Leadanah brought Isor!"

The therios who were not occupied with the wailing woman or the struggling man turned my way eagerly, crying out, "The boy," and "is he alive?"

"He's dead," I told Larson, handing him over.

Larson took the child and lowered him to the ground. He placed a small hairy hand around Isor's wrist and lowered his ear to his mouth.

"He lives!" Larson announced to the crowd. "He's suffered a blow to the head, but he's alive."

There a was a flurry of activity as the wailing woman leaped to her feet and flung herself upon the boy, crying. The male Therio stopped struggling toward the clearing and turned his attention toward the scene before him.

"Release me! My son!" he growled.

Larson stepped back from the child, who at the sound of his parents' voices let out a small moan.

"Has he integrated his human?" Larson asked hurriedly.

"No, not yet!" the male fox therio said.

"Isor, let your human form out, you have to rest."

The boy moaned, "No."

His mother spoke softly to him. I couldn't hear what she said, but the boy responded, "Don't hurt her."

"We're not going to hurt her. You need her to help you heal."

26

The boy whimpered in pain but still refused, claiming in his confusion that they wanted to kill her. The boy had revealed too much while he was vulnerable, unable to cloak his heart. They were like me and Andley. Now that everyone knew, they would kill his human form, perhaps even tonight, after they knew he'd healed enough to survive without her. I watched, horrified, as the foxy features of the cub faded into that of a little girl. She gasped and cried out in terror when she realized she was alone and surrounded by the faces of wild therios.

A dull ache pulsed through me. I turned from the crowd and stepped into the clearing, eyes and ears set upon the ongoing battle. The lion therio clung to Justin's back. Digging his claws deep into his shoulders, his back claws scraped along the back of his muscular thighs. Justin was frantic. He swung the therio side to side, reaching over his head attempting to pull him forward. The reptilian darted forward, stabbing Justin in his lower abdomen. Justin kicked him away, and the therio fell backward.

Dante, who had been thrown to the ground moments before, rose on his mighty back legs. Holding his sword with both hands, he pulled his muscular arms backward and coiled down on his hind legs, putting the full weight of his body behind the sword, ready to thrust it into his enemy. Justin finally freed himself from the clutch of the lion on his back and lifted him overhead, holding the now helpless therio high, squeezing his hips and chest. He began bending the therio as if to break his spine in two and tear him apart. The lion let out anguished roars, and attempted to twist out of the mighty grasp. Dante sprang forth, driving the sword outwards. The point entered Justin's abdomen, stopping at the hilt. His roaring stopped abruptly as he dropped the hapless lion sideways. He fell to the ground and scrambled away from the struggle. Justin grasped the hilt of the sword with one hand and pressed on Dante's neck with the other to drive him back. Blood poured from him, covering Dante's from legs as he kept pushing forwards. His hind quarters strained against the massive weight before him.

The giants grunted and struggled against each other. Dante made a sickening choked noise as he tried to gasp for air. Justin gurgled and blood on poured from his mouth, staining his teeth while he rasped painfully.

Finally, Dante pushed him back and raised his front hooves to Justin's chest, beating him down with powerful thrusts. The firing therio fell backward, releasing Dante's neck to brace himself.

The creature still tried to swing at him, but the light was dying from his eyes even as he did so.

Dante stepped back as Justin fell forwards from his knees. The sword's blade jutted from his back. Justin heaved, each inhale a labor to draw in more life, but it fled further from him with each outward breath. He let out wet moans until stillness took over.

The crowd looked out silently. Dante dropped to his front knees watching, horror-stricken. The muscles in his flanks shivered, and he dropped to the ground as though he could not bear the weight of what had happened. The other two therios came forwards and struggled to turn Justin on his side. The lion therio pulled the sword from his stomach. Blood ran from the wound like a river. The onlookers stepped into the clearing. One took the sword from the lion's grasp and mumbled about cleaning it off. The reptilian placed a hand on Dante's shoulder and bid for him to rise. He led Dante away silently.

"Someone else can deal with the rest mate," he said, loud enough for the others to hear. "We'll have to hold his ceremony on the spot. He's too big to move."

The crowd seemed to awaken then. Those with authority began giving orders to collect firewood and oil. They scurried toward the forest's edge.

"Someone needs to collect the bodies and begin cleaning them. Find their families."

Then Isor's father approached the dead fox and knelt to lift his head. He brushed the ashes from his face.

"Oh, my cub," he choked.

"He saved his brother's life," a kindly woman whispered as she helped him lift the body.

Several therios moved to the languishing black panther, who'd initially tried to save the fox cub.

"You'll be okay. It's already mending. Lay still." A bird like therio patted her hip, stroking the fur there comfortingly.

I watched dispassionately, wondering where the little girl was and what would happen to her at the end of this. I looked to Dante; he was still shaking but his eyes were wild with primal adrenaline. He saw me watching him and turned toward me.

"Go, Randal, I'm ok, just a little excited."

The reptilian exclaimed Dante's heroism, saying that the tribes would honor him after the death ceremonies. Dante looked appreciative, but bade him to go. I watched Dante approach with mild interest.

"Let's go," he said, reaching for me with a bloody hand.

I raised an eyebrow at him.

"What has you, Dante?"

"Death, and fear. I need to fuck you."

I smiled and let him lead me away.

"You were afraid?" I asked still grinning.

"Justin was always a force, but I didn't know how strong a mad therio could be. I've seen the madness overtake someone before but never in a titan. It's a damn shame it happened to him."

"Do many wild therios truly go mad?" I was genuinely curious. "Does it truly come on without warning?"

"You've not witnessed it before? It's not as common as the humans think. The progression is usually slow and well known before they can hurt anyone. I don't think anyone saw it in Justin, though. He'd have been put down well before he could have done this if there were signs, given his strength."

I grunted my understanding.

Many therio were rushing past us in the dark, back to the bloody scene with funerary items. Dante walked silently as we passed more tents and fire pits. From the light of the fire, I could see the scowl between his thick eyebrows and the clenched muscles in the hardline of his jaw. He stared into the night unblinking, rubbing his hands together on a rag, trying to clean the blood from them. He didn't seem aware of the blood drying on his stomach and matting the hair of his forelegs.

"Not all things can be predicted," he mumbled, more to himself than to me.

"Nothing can be," I stated.

"He'd never have hurt a child in his right mind. I'm hopeful for the restfulness of his spirit. The boy, Isor, will live. His brother was young but grown."

Thinking of the little girl, I wondered who the mad ones really were. A sinking sensation, like falling passed through me and my heart thundered. Pushing away the thought of Iso and his human aside, my pace quickened and I stepped in front of Dante, leading him into his caravan as we approached.

For wild therio, their size and ability to fight dictated their status and lifestyle. They lived in what ever shelter they could build. The frail, small therio, rodent types or small reptiles, usually only kept temporary nests, abandoning them as they migrated. Dante's size and shape allowed him to build a much larger caravan to live in than most others. He had more freedom and riches because he could take what he wanted, fight to keep it and also carry what he had on his own. In part, this made him one of the leaders among the wild therio, but mostly his kindness and calm nature made smaller therio look to him.

I slid the heavy curtain aside as I stepped into the wide entrance at the back of his caravan. Within sat a low table with cushions surrounding it. A large wooden mug still half full of tea say upon it. Beside this lay a carving knife and a length of birch, a flute in the making. About the walls and ceiling hung sheer silks and hand-woven tapestries with images of animals woven into them. One portrayed a stag standing in a sunlit background, while another donned a hawk diving with its talons stretched before it. Dante didn't weave all of them, but I could recognize one or two items of his own work.

The caravan smelled of burning wood chips and sun-worn leather, laced with Dante's musk, salty with a faint trace of old grass. There was a small potted tree in the corner under a window. Meticulous braids were carved into its thin trunk and slender fronds with leaves like tear drops hung to the soil from delicate branches.

As he stepped in behind me the muffled knock of his hooves on the rug made the wood floor moan. He pressed lightly on my hips, urging me to the pile of feather cushions and blankets across from the fireplace. I went willingly and lowered myself to the floor, waiting patiently. He released the belts from around his hips, taking the cloth covering away with it. Dante reached around to the side of his equine body, piled the sheath loose and placed it upon a rack mounted to the wall. He examined his hands and made for the discarded rag.

"Leave it." My voice slipped through his rising distress.

Dante held his hands before him once again, deciding if he would obey. He seemed to notice the blood on his body then and dropped his hands down, letting out a low sigh. I shifted to slide my legs beneath me and reached out, beckoning him. He folded his massive stallion frame to the ground, kneeling on his forelegs with his gaze locked on mine. The softness left his eyes brown eyes, filling with a primal hunger.

He reached into my quills and grabbed a fistful, pulling me into him. I barred my teeth in surprise as he bit down on my lower lip. I caressed his chest while allowing him to kiss me. His palm covered my chin, holding me still. My hand slid down the carved muscles beneath his smooth skin tracing the path along his ribcage to the threshold where his manhood extended from the massive form of his equine body. The muscles in his hind quarters twitched and he let out a deep groan as I traced the curve of his shaft, human in form but a stallion's in scale.

I revelled in the way it pulsed beneath my palm. He pressed his palms around the swell of my breasts, where my soft skin was bare of fur or feathers. He slid his thumb beneath the feathers which grew downward, covering my nipples, and rubbed his thumb over them gently. I moved one hand over his and forced his fingers to dig into my skin while stroking him teasingly in long, slow thrusts. I loved that my hand could barely wrap around his full girth. He rocked forward, frustrated at the lightness of my touch. He lifted his hands from my breasts and swept the long quills framing my face to the side, pulling them over one of my shoulders. I sucked in a sharp breath at the unnatural placement. He slapped my hand away from his cock and grasped it at the base.

"You're a fucking brat Leadanah, you know that?"

I laughed and pulled him closer to me, resting one hand on the back of his neck and the other over the one encompassing his cock. He stroked himself a few times, then holding the head steady he thrust himself forwards and into me. I threw my head back and let out a moan mixed with laughter, feeling his length slide into me fully as my body welcomed him.

He slid his hands beneath my thighs and lifted me from my knees, holding my weight. I laced my fingers behind his head and leaned back, relaxing my wings so they dropped to the ground behind me. He bucked up and forced me back down, each arch of his hips crashing into me. My laughter slid into high gasps and moans as I let him take me on how he wanted, riding the wave of his throbbing pleasure until he was spent inside me.

When he was done, he pulled me into him, holding me tightly. One muscular arm barred across my back beneath my wings. I nuzzled my cheek into his neck, kissing his shoulder and ran one hand through his long mane, feeling the rough texture of it through my fingers. We rested together for a time; I rocked my hips slowly along his length, still enjoying the feeling of him inside me. Finally, he gently pulled himself free and handed me a large cloth. I chuckled and began cleaning myself.

Dante stood up and reached his arms overhead, pressing his hands up on the ceiling in a long stretch. I raised an eyebrow, watching him.

"Dante?"

"Yes?" He looked down at me, grinning.

"What will happen to Isor?" The words came out in a slow cadence.

"What do you mean? Isor will be fine. He will miss his brother but—"

"No, I mean when his injuries are healed. He seemed very concerned for his human soul."

"Oh, that. I never realized he still had his human. A little rare, being mixed gendered, I knew one once before though when I was a kid. They will have to help him get rid of her I suppose. It's well past time. He's far too old to still have his human."

"How will they do that? He doesn't seem to want to." My heart was pounding again, and I wished vaguely that I hadn't asked.

Dante looked down at me, frowning, his eyes narrowed.

"I hope they can convince him to do it on his own. It's an awful thing when others have to help. Harder when they are little girls. I can't help with it but there are those who aren't as soft as I am." The heavy muscles in his jaw clenched as he ground his teeth.

"I don't know, aren't there some wild therios who have not destroyed their human side? Surely, he can choose not to."

"What are you talking about?" he asked.

"I'm just saying why does he have to if he does not want to?" I shrugged.

"Sometimes children hold on to their comforts for too long. It's like when you leave a baby to its pacifier, after a while if the child doesn't discard it, the parents must take it away so the child can grow. It hurts for a time, but they forget."

His words struck me. "When did you get rid of your human?"

He raised his eyebrows and looked up. "Oh, it was so long ago, I don't think I remember my age at the time. Maybe I was four?"

"Four?" I gasped. That was young even for humans to complete integration. Do you remember your human?"

"Oh no, we were too young. It's best to do it before you can really get to know it. Why? Do you remember your human?"

I hesitated, careful to choose my next words.

"I do remember her. I was a little like Isor. I didn't want to do it."

Dante nodded. "That surprises me about you, but it's common. If Isor won't do it, the tribe will spare him and do it on his behalf."

"How is that done?"

"Its ugly. They force the human form out and kill it as swiftly as possible. Hopefully, before it knows what's happening." He stared at the wall behind me while he said this.

"Dante, wild animals aren't even that ruthless."

He looked up at me, stricken by this.

"It must be done."

"You must murder children? There aren't many evils that I avoid, but I can't say I'd kill a baby."

"You keep yourself so far from the rest of us, this is why you don't understand." His face was reddening. I wondered if it was from anger or shame.

"When a human won't integrate, they just banish them." My voice was flat.

"Why are you saying these things Leadanah?"

"I hear the grumblings, the complaints. Your people seek acceptance from the humans, to be as you are and pass through their society in peace. I have thought the tribes ill treated. The humans have been wrong to reject you for the madness that takes you. Now I know they were right, if not for the wrong reason."

I rose to my feet and strode to the curtain, pausing before it. Dante's face was a mask of confusion.

"You speak as though you are not one of us."

"I'm not Dante. I don't have any use for humans. They are pretty disgusting creatures. But even they do not kill children. I'm not one of you. And your people should let Isor exist the way he chooses."

"What do you mean by this, Leadanah?"

"He would have been better off dead than condemned to that silence. Maybe it's the silence that drives your people mad," I snapped.

"Leadanah, do you still share your body with your human soul?"

I pulled the curtain back and looked over my shoulder at him. Dante's eyes were wide and his mouth gaped, already knowing the answer.

"I do."

"Wait, don't go yet!" he shouted, reaching for me as I stepped off the caravan and shot upwards. "Leadanah, come back!"

My wings carried me above the encampment, and I turned back toward the forest. I looked down at Dante's caravan and saw him staring up at me, helpless as I shrunk from his view. I doubted I'd see him again. I wasn't sure if it bothered me. Dante was better than the rest of them. But that didn't mean he was good. He was no better than me or anyone else.

I found the stream and washed the blood out of my fur and the cum from my thighs. I spent the rest of the night hunting and made my way back to the castle as the sun was coming up.

My way back into the castle was easier than when I'd left. I slipped silently through the corridors and into the bed without incident, resolving to keep the whole ordeal of the night to myself. It wasn't Andley's concern.

Chapter 3
Andley

"Rise and shine, Lady Andley."

Marlette pulled the curtain back from my bed and the heat within swirled with the fresh cool air caressing my exposed breast causing goosebumps all over my body. I curled up onto my side, wrapping one wing around my naked body.

"Leadanah?" I said inwardly.

Leadanah groaned sleepily. She stretched out and receded back, taking our wings with her. My own body took the place of Leadanah's therio features as I stood up and wrapped a green silk robe around my shoulders.

"Still so modest, my lady," said Marlette. "Some would say you ought to have outgrown it by now. It won't serve you during the ceremony."

She disappeared briefly beside the bed and rose with the fallen sheets.

"You see my lady, all around you our nature is present. Why do you cringe away so?" she asked, walking the sheets to the laundry basket.

I looked around the room and took in the images I usually ignored. All around were carved reliefs of the male power along with females pleasuring it, or themselves upon it. Figures of varying forms were carved into the wood walls engaged in all positions a beast or human could imagine. As the winged therios rose from the center of the wall, their intimate acts became more exclusive to single partnerships or equal giving of pleasures, but soon, if the eye was keen, one would notice that subtly the images changed as the eye rose upwards.

The figures nearest to the ceiling were depicted in the most holy forms of beasts, mainly those with functional wings. There were fewer males depicted with more females writhing upon them. The most debased pleasures were nearest the floor. These figures engaged in pain and blood. If one looked closely, they would see the beasts were killing each other with their desires. I wondered again why there were no figures who seemed to derive pleasure from pleasuring each other.

All are expected to take part in harems such as that carved on the wall, aiming always for the highest level of status with the rarest and most devoted collection. Strong alliances are made when kingdoms can trade beautiful women or men of uncommon therio types to the harems of nobility. Those whose therios are rare types such as ones with wings or those that are water types are most valuable and achieve high status for the masters of their harem. It can be very unfortunate however, for those who are rare but not of nobility. They are sold and traded time and time again, but gain no status. Often, they end up in noble houses as party favors, used until they are no longer beautiful.

The noble man who owns the harem may collect as many as he'd like and can support, but he may also mate outside of the harem, whereas the people within the harem are forbidden from mating with anyone but the head of the harem.

Sometimes, if a female has a high rank coming from a powerful family, she can create boundaries such as I shall have you nine times out of ten. Or you may only have this many, or you will not have that one. It depends however, on the level of power that female brings to the male and what the cost of offending her may be. Very, very few females are allowed even a single consort, and even then, open display of this often leads to punishment or even death, depending on the power of the male's house and the level of shame it brings for others if she is found out.

My stomach sank as I thought of this. I knew the Prince allowed none of his mates to have a consort. Leadanah would never adhere to it. I thought back to our youth when Leadanah attempted to make a male adhere to her alone. It was madness. Just completely left of the path. I had watched from the back of her mind, one of the rare occasions I'd been conscious when she was in control.

I watched her straddled over the rogue therio. He'd been large, fierce and strong. Leadanah enjoyed him very much and often. The two had a long, and I'd say, a serious courtship. Growling down at him, she said that if he thought she would stop having others, then he must as well. The male had laughed, as many others would have, surely. She tore him up after the first guffaw escaped his mouth. Through her eyes, I watched as she rose, her silver furred breast running red, leaving him whimpering in pain. I watched as he lay sprawled out, struggling to rise. She turned and never looked back while she ascended. She never returned to check on his condition. When Leadanah is done with someone, it is total. To this day, I am not certain if he lived.

"My lady?"

I snapped back as the sound of Marlette's irritated voice intruded on my pondering.

"My lady, are you listening to me?" she asked, her voice taut and lips turned down.

"No, Marlette, I am not. What do you need? I am tired and feeling like poor company."

I turned and looked at her cooly. My jaw slackened with surprise when I saw she was standing at the wardrobe holding up two gowns.

"I need nothing my lady. It is you who needs to choose a traveling dress. The Prince's party will be here for you in mere hours. His message was that you may choose between the colors green or red for your travel wear."

Her voice cracked, and she dropped her eyes, trying to hide the tears sliding down her cherub cheeks. My own eyes widened. Hot tears spilled out of me like a breaking dam. At the same time, a rage rolled through me like a smoldering fire in the roots of the forest.

"He permits me to choose my own clothing? I will wear pants," I hissed.

"My lady." There was a sternness in her voice only Rathon had ever directed toward me. "What has gotten into you? I know it must be hard. It will take time to adjust, but he is your mate. You must obey. Why do you choose now, at this stage of your life, to be rebellious? Requesting to skip the consummation ceremony? Refusing him your therio? Now this! My lady, do you not know the situation you are in? The situation the whole tribe faces? The dire need of every person living in this forest?" Her small, meek human form was rapidly being replaced by her therio, which while still small and foxlike, took on a snarling wild demeanor. "You will kill us all, Andley! Do you mean to? We are at war!" she cried. "The lower classes are starving. Our lives are riding on you and your rarity and the influence your house holds!"

She was yelling at me by the time she finished. I had never seen her behave this way. She stopped, abruptly realizing herself.

"My lady," she whispered.

Marlette hung her head again and fought with herself to regain her human form while tears fell from her hidden face. My face grew hot with shame.

My tribe is filled with mighty warriors, and we have a large, elite army, but we cannot force our way into the canalizing mountain range that encompasses the valley, nor can we draw them into open plains of the valley to destroy them with brute force. As their forces have pushed further into our territory occupying the canopy of the forest, the people have run out of food and have been displaced, migrating deeper and closer to the center city of the forest. If the situation persisted, our people would starve before our army could push them back.

To end the attrition of Brath's aggression, Rathon was forced to sign onto a treaty with the kingdom of Sandor, who once occupied our forest and subjugated us, in exchange for food and clean water from the rivers bordering our kingdoms. Along with access to the rivers, King Mesck gave thousands of troops to push back Brath's army.

Rathon believed the end goal for Sandor was Brath becoming one of their colonies, using us to subjugate them. Within the treaty, we agreed to respond to any call to war from Sandor, repayment of the value of all troops lost in the fight, and to pay an ongoing tax for as long as we access their waters. To pay for the food and ratify the agreement, I was to be gifted to Prince Marston, to become part of his harem as his head mate.

"Marlette, I am, I am ashamed. Please forgive me. I have behaved like a spoiled pup." Bowing low, I exposed the back of my neck to her for the second time in less than a day.

Her skirts rustled as she came to me and cupped the back of my neck with chilled fingers. A gesture of affection and forgiveness. I had honestly expected the hard slap. Servants only had to serve, not love us. Reprimands were permitted and commonplace if their master insulted them; forgiveness wasn't expected. The last time Marlette reprimanded me, Rathon had commanded her. She wrapped me so hard with her clawed hand it had bruised, and I couldn't turn my head for several days. I'd been such a spoiled child.

I looked up and saw her crystal blue eyes, wide and timid. She was crying openly now as she struggled to take on her human form. Marlette always maintained dignified control, the serving class's point of pride. It was so odd to see her struggling with control.

"My lady, Andley, we love you. The King loves you. None of us want this. We are selling our own princess. You act this way before me because I know you. I have always known you. But do not do this to the others, you will wound them." Her voice shook slightly as she regained composure.

"Forgive me, Marlette. I will compose myself; I will not shame them. Please. I am sorry," I begged.

For the first time since our youth, I embraced Marlette, and we held each other like sisters.

***

I wore an evergreen gown to match the home I was leaving. The skirt flowed down my sleek legs, ending conservatively at my pointed toes, brushing the grass daintily. It had long sheer and silky golden sleeves. They ended in tight cuffs, buttoning elegantly at my wrists. In stark contrast, the neckline plunged dramatically between my breasts, stopping scandalously beneath my navel, leaving fully half of my chest exposed. Delicate, ornate wooden beads were laced loosely across the gap. Carved upon them were tiny lilies. These types of beads are exceptionally rare, carved by hand with the most delicate tools by a master carver specifically for the wearer. Why Prince Marston of Brath sent me beads with such a powerful symbolism, I could not grasp. Surely it was a message for me only. Maybe lilies represented something else in Brath, but in my own culture they symbolized the beauty and brevity of life's everlasting cycle of life and death. We can barely take in its beauty before it wilts away, but hope remains, for a new blossom will soon come. Perhaps the Prince just thought women liked lilies.

The beads were sent to me at the signing of the treaty. I'd have been delighted with such a treasure if things were different. Historically, beads such as these were worn by a woman to express her desire for the affection of a lover. He is meant to lean in to examine the special details carved upon them, an intimate and private encounter meant only for him. Typically, though, they are given to brides to wear on the first occasion she will meet her new mate. I am often horrified to know how traditions become deformed by the convenient interpretations of those in power. Once a romantic and intimate gesture between lovers, becomes an empty formality and a symbol of, what? Control? Ownership? I couldn't quite form the feeling into a coherent thought, but it disgusted me regardless.

I followed the stone path out from the shade of the last tree, stepping into the glade where Rathon waited for me to be taken away. The nobles and lords of the court, all the most important people of the tribes and forest, trailed somberly behind me. They stopped within the edge of the tree line as though hesitant to expose themselves to the open sky, while I carried on alone.

Black eyed Susan's grew defiantly where the cart track cut deep into the soil. It ran through the center of the clearing, glinting in the sunlight. There are few steel structures in the forest. Everything we have built is from the forest itself and constantly groomed by hand until there it no more use of it, that way the forest can take back its place when we have moved on.

Rathon had stopped short of having the track destroyed after the rebellion. However, since negotiations with Sandor began, workers cleared away the overgrowth.

Leadanah waited awake within. She was oddly aroused, excited at the prospect of leaving the vast wilderness of the forest. In her mind, we were visiting the city. She thought she would leave whenever she became bored.

Rathon stood in his dimidium, facing north where the Prince's delegation would appear. He held his gaze down the track, careful not to look at me. I stood beside him and also took up watching the cart track.

"You look beautiful, my lady," he said, his voice hollow.

I flinched. My lady.

"Rathon." I looked up at him while his stare remained firm. "Must I be a lady with you today?"

"This is a dignitary delegation." His tone was weary. "The nobles are watching. Please, spare me more suffering."

He shifted, his leg twitching. His fingers flexed at his sides, fighting the need to scratch at the fabric of his formal attire.

"This skirt is unbearable."

I smiled, though my chest ached. "How do you know I am beautiful? You have not looked at me."

His jaw clenched. "I have looked upon you." His voice softened. "You just didn't see."

His chin dipped, the movement slight, almost imperceptible. As he spoke, his eyes shifted downward, barely meeting mine before darting away.

"You look lovely," he said, more firmly this time, as if bracing himself. "The Prince will be pleased."

My eyebrow cocked upwards as an involuntary sneer twitched upon my lips.

"I did not dress to please the Prince." My voice was barely a whisper. I stepped closer. "Won't you look more closely upon me?"

His breath stilled. Then his lips parted, and his voice, low and raw, brushed my ear, weighted with something unspoken.

"Why?" he murmured. "Do you wish to see my suffering?"

I froze. The weight of my selfishness pressed into my ribs. What was I doing?

"I'm sorry, Rathon," I whispered.

His fingers curled into fists. His shoulders rose with a breath, then fell again. When he next spoke, his voice dropped to a low gravel deep in his chest to force down the trebling that had nearly escaped with his words, burying it deep where neither of us could reach.

"I wish we could be alone, Andley. Then I would tell you all that I feel."

I wanted to say something. Anything. The Prince's delegation appeared like a mirage glinting in the sunlight. I turned to look at Rathon, my king, guardian, and best friend.

He had a plain wolf type therio, like the rest of his blood tribe, but he was magnificent, nonetheless. He stood tall on his wolfish legs, his tail hanging limp beneath the traditional mesh grass skirt that sat low on his hips, fluttering in the breeze. His fur glimmered where the sunlight caught it. His chest, still that of a man, was covered in white fur that stretched over his shoulders and down between his pectoral muscles like a draped cloak.

Rathon's features were wolfish, but distinctly his own. His speckled nose extended slightly into a short muzzle, his velvety ears protruding from his thick black hair. They were pulled downward, along with the corners of his mouth. Rathon's hand clutched his ceremonial spear so tightly his claws dug into his palm. His broad shoulders were stiff, yet he leaned into the spear as though needing its support. His biceps bunched and the muscles in his forearm seemed as taut as a rope as he grasped the shaft of his ceremonial spear. Rathon's sharp yellow eyes stared soberly into the distance down the road.

I looked around us, as if to show him no one had come up beside us.

"No one can hear us Rathon," I teased

He looked down and glared at me. "I will be glad to no longer endure your torments," he hissed.

I blinked, the shadow of his stare settling over me like a cloud blocking the sun.

"That was hurtful." My voice was small. I hadn't meant to sound so amused.

I could feel the loss of him already. We had a strange relationship. In the beginning, we were nothing more than two noble children growing up within the court, with no reason to interact. His father was the duke, reigning over all the forest, and mine was a noble of the highest house and one of his advisers. We both, in our own way, held some of the highest seats in our tribe by virtue of our birth.

My father and mother were envoys to Sandor, sent to deliver our conditions for a ceasefire. They were killed on the road by bandits. Or so they deduced. After they died, Rathon's family adopted me. Then, when Rathon's own father died of injuries he suffered from battle, he inherited his title. Rathon's rage had shaken the forest loose from its enemies. Where his father had refused to use savage tactics, Rathon had embraced them and in doing so, he won us the right to call ourselves a kingdom. He was made king, and I became his ward.

Resentment and rage suddenly overwhelmed me.

"I am feeding our people with my body—sold to the Prince like cattle, expected to warm his bed and bear his heirs in exchange for their safety. Do you ever think of that?"

A cruel thing to say. Rathon had been everything. My friend. My protector. The one who kept me when I had no one. He never hurt me. Never took me. I met his gaze again. A terrible longing crept through me—one I had no right to feel. His golden eyes burned brighter and to my horror, they filled with tears.

"No Rathon, I am sorry. I didn't … Please don't, I don't know what's come over me lately," I cried out, no longer caring if the other nobles heard me.

I reached for him, but he snatched my wrist with his free hand and held it at bay. Tears were threatening to spill over like soldiers falling from a wall.

Oh, no please, I thought. I did not think I could bear to be the cause of this mighty warrior falling from such a height. He called out loudly, so all the others could hear.

"The Lady Andley requires discipline. She is forgetting her place and must be reminded before she goes to live among our neighbors, lest she shames us."

I was horrified. He's never struck me. There was an audible gasp followed by worried murmuring from within the tree line.

"Rathon!" I sputtered. Trying to wrench my wrist free from his grasp.

"Leave us wholly. All of you, I will not strike her before your eyes," he called out.

His body jerked violently, muscles locking as he shifted into his therio. There was no slow, creeping change; no warning. His bones cracked like splitting wood, the force of his transformation rippling outward. Fur burst from his skin as his frame expanded, surging larger, wilder. His face contorted, jaw jutting forward as his teeth elongated into daggers. His ears flicked up sharply.

There was a frantic rustling as the party behind us hastily withdrew. Although he held my wrist immobile for the duration, his grasp was almost gentle, his claws barely pressing into my forearm. His touch was so light, yet so strong. I could not move my arm even an inch.

"Parkab," he called out. "Make sure they are all away."

I jolted as Parkab emerged from the tall grass, barely fifteen feet from where Rathon and I stood. He was in his therio form—another wolf type. But unlike most when in their therio form, he shed every trace of his human self. He moved low and seamless, dropping onto all fours with the precision of a true predator. Every inch of him mimicked a gray wolf perfectly, not just in shape, but in the way he carried himself.

Parkab, like the rest of Rathon's inner pack, had been trained to master his form so completely that they were indistinguishable from a real wolf pack. He let out a sharp yip of acknowledgment before vanishing into the trees. Moments later, the howls and cries of the rest of the pack rang through the forest, carrying out his orders, urging the crowd away. The annoyed shouts of noblemen faded. There would be no stragglers.

Faithful Parkab, never asked why, never told a secret. He was Rathon's most trusted commander and friend. I knew he would never disobey to Rathon's, nor tell anyone what he did to me.

I crouched into a bow. Surprised outrage rippled through me as I submitted my neck to Rathon's coming wrath.

45

Rathon stared down at me as I attempted to bow. He dropped the ceremonial spear and with his hand free he reached beneath my chin. He grabbed my throat, cradling my jaw in the pad of his hand and held it up, forcing me to look upon him. His stare shattered my heart, and my breath caught. I struggled against him, trying to pull my wrist free of his grasp. I looked up and found his golden eyes had become their pale ocean blue green again. His rage seemed to drain from him with the tears spilling down his rough cheeks. I continued my fruitless effort to flee, nonetheless.

"Don't," he whispered hoarsely. "Just stop pulling away from me."

As his anger subsided, he slipped into his human form, finally allowing himself to shed his king's mask and just be Rathon.

He dropped my wrist and put his forearm behind my waist, pulling me close to him. His grip on my chin softened as he caressed my throat and then my cheek. My heart fluttered madly. I felt Leadanah politely turn away and disconnect her mind from my own.

Rathon's brow furrowed as he leaned into me, the intensity of his eyes holding my own. His lips parted and met mine. We held each other there. I wished we could become stone and never have to leave or move or see anyone in the world ever again. It was my single greatest longing since I was a little girl. This moment, the happiest and most terrible. My heart tore itself apart, and at the same time all the wounds of my longing knitted together and healed. God, why now? When it is too late for us, I thought in agony.

The wooden beads pressed into my flesh as he pushed my body into his. I was astonished as the skin of my breast pressed into his bare chest. Never before had we made physical contact with our skin touching, we had never even touched hands. I was shocked; he had always felt so close to me, yet I never noticed the lack of physical contact. I sobbed and pulled away, overwhelmed.

"Rathon, I want this, but I can't." My voice caught.

"I can't either."

He drew my face back to his with a firm gentleness. He kissed me again and began running his hands through my long, colorful hair.

"Never the same," he muttered. "Every time I look upon you, you are never the same. Your hair, your eyes, the way you walk, your smile. You're new every time I see you. I can never look at you twice."

My hands, which had been cradling his back clenched at his words, digging my fingertips into the space between his shoulder blades. His voice alone made me want to moan with pleasure. No words had ever affected me like that before.

"I was always waiting. Why do you come to me now? I have to go," I whispered.

"Please, Andley. I must tell you what is in my heart. Will you hear me?" he asked.

I nodded. Still holding him, caressing the muscles along his back. Up and down, savoring his warmth, his strength. Imprinting the texture of his skin into my mind.

He paused and looked unsure, shy even, for the first time in his life. "I mean it. I have never seen you twice. You are always a marvel, new to me. When we were children, I would see you and not recognize you at first. It was like seeing a glimmer of light. It is always there, but it never shines the same way. I never took a mate, even when my advisers told me to start my harem. I just never wanted one. I don't want one."

My thoughts ceased racing as it occurred to me what he might be saying.

He can't mean that. He's not a fairy tale, I thought.

"I don't understand Rathon, you have had many women. What do you mean?" I asked.

"I could have you, or I could have had you, and been satisfied. Fulfilled. I know it," he stated it as though it was the only truth he ever had to tell.

Hot tears fell from my eyes and landed on my chest, mingling with his.

"I never knew. If I had known, Rathon, I would never have," I stammered. "I'd have done things differently."

I thought of Leadanah and was grateful she was gone for the moment, for the thought I had she would not have liked.

"You have a double meaning in that," he said.

He suddenly held me away and looked so deeply into me I felt as though I was caught naked in the light. All I could do was stare back. How could he know? I wondered. He can't possibly.

"You have not integrated your therio. We know, Marlette and I," he said.

I froze, the breath within me hung like air in a jar.

The stories always ended the same way. Banishment, madness and death. A creature that no longer recognized itself as anything but hunger and rage. The more intelligent, the more sadistic. We keep the therio's mind independent only long enough that it can strengthen us when we integrate it. But to let it grow into itself is to risk losing the human mind to it. At least this is what we believe happens when the therio takes over. But Leadanah wasn't mad. She wasn't an animal clawing blindly at the walls of my mind.

"No," I whispered, disbelieving. "How can you ..."

"We're your friends Andley. We have grown up together. Marlette practically raised us both. You can't hide yourself so completely." He smiled.

Before I could speak, he pulled me back into himself and this time his tenderness subsided only a little with earnest. I held him closer while we kissed. He pressed his whole body against mine and I felt him through the thin silk of my gown. I had chosen it for its color; it reminded me of the forest, and I knew Rathon favored green. Its scant design and thin materials had dismayed me. Now I was grateful for its thin, sheer silkiness. Grateful now for its open plunging front, for the feeling of his skin on my skin; for his heat mixing with mine.

My breath became short, and as my excitement threatened to overcome me. He began making small, steady thrusting movements with his hips into me. I put my hand on his hip and felt the muscles flexing there with each small movement. Both of us wanted more. He placed a large, calloused hand between my breasts and found the wooden beads there, blocking his way. I felt his hatred for what it symbolized as he closed his fist around the wire and tore it away. The beads flew from me and scattered to the ground.

"Never wear those for him," he said. An order I was finally pleased to obey.

48

He plunged his hand into the bodice of my dress and held it over my breast for a moment, feeling my hard nipple beneath his large palm before stopping and looking up, as though seeking something. He lifted my legs and wrapped them around his waist. Then he lifted me up and walked toward the tree line.

When he found a spot with deep shadows, he bent down and placed me on the soft, moss-filled ground. We had somehow found a rare niche in the forest, where darkness and moisture met perfectly to create a cave like effect in the decaying dead fall around us. The light glowed around us, causing a melancholy halo effect around his gleaming body.

He stood briefly, taking a final look around to see that we were alone. I gazed up at him from my knees. His body was gleaming in the dimness, and I realized we were surrounded by glowing dead wood. Of all the world's little miracles, bioluminescence has always been my favorite. I could see it a thousand times and still feel like it's the first time; like I could never see it twice. The connection tore through me with devastating realization. We would never be like this again. How many years might pass before we would meet again? Would we be filled with loss instead of desire? Will we be strangers by then?

He seemed to tower over me kneeling before him and reaching his waist, my hands shaking, grasping the grass skirt, eager to tear it from his body. I halted, drawing in a steadying breath, stark reality reminding me he would have to redress later. My fingers curled around the hemp string holding it on instead and the skirt fell to the ground. He was staring down at my upturned face, a nervous smirk twitching at the corn of his mouth. Our faces must have been mirrors of surprise at the moment he was exposed. Heat radiated from him as my cheeks flushed. He raised one strong arm and ran his fingers through his hair, watching me intently. His chest rose and fell in rapid, shallow breaths.

He reached behind himself. His fingertips met the wall of stone behind us, and finding purchase, calmed a little.

Giving pleasure with a mouth full of sharp teeth wasn't something often practiced, even with familiar mates. It is never offered for the want of doing

49

it. Typically, the act is demanded by a conqueror or master to exert control over submissive mates or a defeated enemy.

For the first time in a long time, I felt nervous with him. His phallus was already erect, and it surprised me for a moment. I sucked in a little breath of air and gazed at it. I had always imagined myself and him together, but I could never bring myself to be so vulgar as to fantasize so directly about his manhood. I had not prepared myself for the actual sight of him. It stood to his bellybutton, curving gently inwards, nearly touching it. The large vein running along its underside bulged slightly, wanting to be caressed. I followed its inviting line to the head and saw the subtle change in his skin color there were the swelling and pulsing of the blood had gathered into a slight rosiness.

The head was already glistening in wet anticipation. I reached out, my fingers gently curved and grazed the base before I slid them to the top. It stirred under my touch. I moved my forefinger to the head of his penis and slid it around with the clear wetness there, causing him to shiver slightly.

"Mmm," he hummed quietly.

My eyes fluttered upward to his face. He was looking down at me with a soft grin. I used my finger to press the throbbing head against his lower abdomen and firmly ran my fingers up and down the outside edge of it from the top, just beneath the shaft. It throbbed again, releasing more sweet wetness. I'd never experienced pre-cum this early before. Just the idea of my mouth had gotten him this excited. I imagined how it might feel on my tongue, and my mouth salivated a little. Acting on the urge, I leaned forward, sticking out the tip of my tongue, intending to lick it teasingly. I started at the base and slid it slowly up his shaft, giving it a final slow flick at the top. He groaned again.

"Yes," he said, excited.

I repeated the motion a few more times and eventually I had my whole tongue licking and gliding up and down while he pressed his hips forward, wanting more. He reached out and dug his fingers into my hair, grabbing it firmly without pulling.

"Good girl," he said, his voice husky.

I felt a surge of warmth run through my groin at that and knew I was getting wet. I parted my lips and pressed them over the head of his cock. I slid down to the bottom edge of it massaging with my tongue. I wondered if he knew how much I was enjoying keeping him in anticipation. I closed my lips around his girth and began sucking and massaging it from the base of his cock to its swelling tip. I moved my head up and down slowly, but earnestly. His grasp on my hair tightened, and he began making small thrusting movements into me. I pressed both my hands on his hip bones and held them back. As though taking a cue, he leaned back and sought the wall of the rock behind him so he could lean on it.

I moved faster, and at the bottom of each stroke, I pressed the head harder to the back of my throat, forcing it further down each time. I wondered how it would feel with the tightness of my throat encompassing his cock, squeezing it while he thrusted, what it might be like to feel him throbbing there as he came. More wetness pulsated from me at the idea. I had never imagined liking it this much or wanting to do so many things to him with my mouth.

Little groans escaped him gently with every quick movement of my mouth sliding along him, and I could feel little warm spurts of his pre-cum hitting the back of my throat. I made my way back to the head of his cock slowly easing off the intensity of my motions. When I could feel its pulsing beat behind my lips, I pressed it gently between the roof of my mouth and my tongue making a short steady rocking motion, only ever allowing it to enter part way. His moans intensified, and he grabbed his cock at the base, squeezing it and rubbing it in a short upward motion as though willing it forward so I would take more of him in. I reached out and replaced his hand with my own. It was slick with my saliva, and I savored the feeling of his warm skin moving over that marble like hardness. I rubbed it lightly, still wanting him to wait for more.

I released him from my mouth so I could watch my hands glide along his length. When I realized my small hands couldn't wrap around his girth, I took it with both. I looked up at him and saw he was watching my hands with a vague look of smirking satisfaction. The aching between my legs

51

grew and my nipples pressed harder against my dress, as though my body were calling and reaching for his cock to be inside. He let his head fall back as his passionate sighs became low, sultry grunts. His hips were thrusting rhythmically.

As wonderful of a sight it was, I knew if I didn't slow down, it would be over before I had everything; I wanted from him. I slowed the rhythm of my hands and kissed the head of his cock, lightly caressing it with my lips. He put a hand in my hair again, pulling my head back softly.

I leaned back, resting on my calves, still massaging him lightly. I looked up at him questioning, but before I could say anything more he leaned forward and, pushing himself over top of me, forced me on my back.

He placed his hand around the back of my head, cushioning it as I went down. His kiss was intense as he pressed himself against my body. His tongue slipped between my lips and caressed my own. Soon his powerful hand was slipping gently into my bodice. The callouses on his palms grazed against my skin as he cupped the swelling of my breast. My whole body flushed with the pleasure of his warm hands, and I absentmindedly stroked the muscles between his shoulder blades. I could feel his manhood pressing against me through the thin silk dress. He removed his hand from my breast to slide the sleeve off my shoulder, exposing me to the crisp air. He leaned forward again and kissed me. This time, I could feel his teeth grazing my lips and his nails digging slightly into my skin. As though he hoped to ravage me as gently as possible. He pressed his mouth onto my neck and bit down, careful not to leave a mark, mixing the slightest pain with my pleasure.

How would it be if when the Prince laid himself on me at the ceremony and he saw the marks of someone else covering my body? I suddenly wished that Rathon's gentleness would cease, and he really would bite me and tear into my smooth flesh, to make me his before he gave me away.

His kisses were working hungrily down my neck. He ran the tip of his tongue from the bottom swell of one breast to the tip of my nipple. My body responded with the same wanting shudder as though he'd touched me below. Soon his lips were working upon it, and I felt his teeth graze me there too.

I moaned, "Bite me, Rathon."

"Shhhh," he responded. "Why do you torment me with things I cannot do?"

He kissed me again with his light caressing lips and bit down on me a little harder, sucking the tender skin before releasing it. The control he displayed over his own desire sent me further into my lust; I squirmed and raised myself into him, wanting more.

He pulled the dress off my other arm, the light silk slid smoothly across my body like cool water. Exposed and unguarded now, he went to work, teasing, biting, caressing and licking all over my breasts, moving methodically down my stomach to where the plunging neckline ended, below my belly button. He reached up with one hand, running it along the curvature of my waistline, feeling the length between my hip and ribs, stopping at the height of my ribcage. He squeezed, digging his nail into my skin tearing at it in a slow drag. At the same time, he glanced up at me and pulled the sash from around my waist, loosening it from the only place it was still fastened to me. I lifted my hips as he worked the dress down.

Once I was free of the gown, he sat upright, towering over me, looking down upon my now fully naked body. I gazed back up at him through the blue light, watching his chest rise and fall with every quick, shallow breath. His muscular thighs pressed down on mine, holding me still. My eyes wandered down his muscular body to his hard cock. A cold breeze passed between us and goosebumps rose all over my flesh.

I wanted his warmth on me, to feel his naked skin on mine. Rathon leaned forward again and simultaneously moved one of his knees between mine – gently, almost politely, spreading them apart. Next, he placed his other knee inside and it was now my shaking legs which held him. He kissed my inner thigh as he slid downward. I drew in rapid breaths, not believing what he was about to do. I felt his lips graze the soft flesh just above my clit. He kissed around it gently and I let out an excited whimper that I couldn't hold in.

"Andley," he whispered. His voice had a hint of delight.

He pressed my hips down, holding me still as his kiss finally pressed down on the aching pulsing spot, like a cooling relief. Rathon began sucking gently, pulling slightly upwards at each release. He did this smoothly and slowly as my hips tried to thrust upwards in time, all the while he firmly held me in place. He slid his tongue beneath my clit, moving across the swelling flesh there. He grazed lightly along up and down, alternating his kissing lips with his sliding tongue. All the while, he whispered my name every so often in a voice so low and deep I could hardly hear it.

"Rathon," I nearly sobbed.

My moans became light musical notes, pulsating out of me at each stroke, like I'd become his instrument.

His tongue found its way inside me, just at the entrance, and pushed lightly in and out. I reached down, squeezing his shoulders, and my hands ran through his hair, stroking him mindlessly. I could feel the pressure mounting in me as my pleasure grew with every slow, steady flick of his tongue.

He worked methodically, rhythmically. His hand slid past my thigh and with his fingers he reached up into me, pressing steadily. I covered my mouth to muffle the cries of pleasure. Finally, there was a rush pulsing from my clit and radiating throughout my body like a wave. The walls of my vagina constricted around his fingers in a rapid pulse. He pushed his fingers deeper into me, never letting up as I plummeted into an orgasm.

He sat upright again, watching me writhe within myself as he circled the outer edge of my clit lightly with his thumb, drawing out all the pleasure. Still watching me intently, a small grin appeared on his sharp features. He pressed his hand around my throat, squeezing gently. I raised my hands up and ran them along his flexing forearm. He thrust his whole body into me and replaced his fingers with his cock inside me. All at once, feeling his naked body against mine, my orgasm began again. Tears welled in my eyes as though the ecstasy of him inside me created so much pressure that it had to escape.

He grunted a low growl as though his therio would take over. His thrusting became more intense and urgent as he rocked in and out of me. Each time he did this a fresh wave crashed through me, forcing more cries of pleasure from my throat. I had never felt this sensitive inside before. No one had ever made me cum first, then pleasured themselves upon my orgasm.

"Fuck, Andley," he rasped.

"Don't stop, please, please," I begged.

He moved slowly, as though savoring the sliding movements inside me.

"Are you going to cum?" asked

"Mhm." His voice was guttural.

"I want to feel you," I told him.

He pressed forward and up, as though trying to lift my body with the strength of his cock. I placed my hand on his pelvic bone, running it lightly up and down feeling all the involuntary flexing of his muscles as he began to cum.

I gasped as his penis throbbed inside me, feeling him surge and fill me. The sensation caused another rush through me, and I felt myself tightening around him. Our breathing matched the pulsating of his orgasm in short rasps. It went on, seemingly endless, before it slowed and ebbed to a stop.

When it was finally over, he relaxed and kissed me while making light slow thrusts inside me still. I wrapped my hands around his back, massaging him again, and he ran his hands in my hair and along my cheekbones, cupping my chin, kissing me tenderly.

When we finished basking in the afterglow of what we'd done, he handed me my dress shyly. I took it and quietly stood up. Shaking slightly, I strolled to the small stream running lazily a few meters in front of us. The clear water was glacial compared to the heat coming off my body. I washed everything away, sitting on my knees and humming with satisfaction.

Rathon's eyes rested on me, like the hot sun warming my back. I washed my breasts, arms and neck, hoping to rinse away the smell of sex. I found that it also excited me to have done this thing now, when it was more forbidden than ever, rather than earlier when it wouldn't have caused much more than some scandalous gossip. I imagined us carrying out this affair in the coming years. Rathon coming to the palace as an ally of the King, all the while fucking me in dark corridors and smirking at each other knowingly when the Prince could not see. I felt a smirk curving mischievously on my lips.

An earnest voice came suddenly from the depth of the tree line.

"My lord Rathon, the Prince's party is arriving."

I crouched down into the water, trying to hide myself. Reality forced itself on me as I remembered the danger of being caught even now. I covered myself, looking back to where I thought the voice came from.

"There is no need to fear, my lady. I did not look upon you." Parkab's voice was soft and kind.

"There is little time, my lord, but you are not in danger."

I lingered in the stream for a moment, giving Parkab time to leave. Shaking out my gown out my gown, I watched grass fly from its folds. I stepped into it through the top, pulling it upwards over my round hips. Rathon handed me the silk sash as I pulled the rest of my clothing together and adjusted my hair. We walked silently back to the clearing. As we stepped into the sunny clearing, back to the stone pathway, Rathon merged himself to his half form once again adopting both the features of a man and a therio.

"Will you visit me?" I asked quietly.

"I must wait for the King to call me to counsel first, but yes I will visit you," he said, looking down at me kindly.

"Maybe it will be fun," I teased.

He grinned.

"Maybe it will be," he agreed.

We both turned our heads abruptly Rathon's ear turning simultaneously toward the sound of Prince Maston's delegation approaching. It was rowdy with the sound of revelry and music and the high persistent squeaking of wheels on the stone. Rathon turned back to me with a withering look of worry and sadness.

"I will be okay, Rathon," I said.

He pulled me into himself and held me tight.

"I am sending you away with my heart," he said, pulling away. "I pray you never forgive me for selling you to our enemies.

"I have a duty for our people too, Rathon. If my freedom is the cost for their lives, it is the Prince and his father who are slavers. Not you."

At that moment, the first cart turned the bend into the clearing. Rathon looked forward sternly, his grasp on his spear tightened. The only manifestation of his rage. I watched the muscles straining in his forearm, admiring his fur glimmering in the sunlight.

"Andley," he started

"Yes?"

"You're, uh, you're standing too close," he finished in a defeated sort of whisper.

"Oh." My voice was small as I moved away.

Two columns of mounted escorts passed us, followed by the largest caravan I had ever seen. I stared in wonder at the dozen horses trotting in their harnesses. The bear of Sandor's royal family, house Arktos, was branded into the flank of each horse. The caravan itself was decorated with riches and carvings. I thought it was a gross display of decadence. Was paint not efficient to display the house crest? Were the many rumors of poverty amount the citizens of Sandor not true? I had heard that people often choose between paying their rent and buying bread. I made another vow that if I ever gained influence as the high-mate, I'd put an end to that.

There was a loud burst of feminine giggling from within the carriage, followed by a playful growl and more loud giggling screams. The doormen hadn't even finished lining up to announce the Prince before the wooden door burst open and two barely dressed women nearly fell from the top step.

"Oh, goodness! Kandrah!" One of the women gasped clutching the other to stop herself from toppling over.

The other woman paused, her smile only faltering for a moment.

"My prince! Oh, we have preceded you! Your new mate is here before us," she shouted jovially.

A man's voice called out, "Be polite."

She slid the shoulder of her gown up, covering her exposed breast and held her friend's hand as she began her descent down the high steps, letting their grasp go on the way down.

"Darling, she is darling. Oh my, this is so rude of us," she said laughing still.

I wondered if they were drunk. She glided to the bottom of the stairs, stepping daintily as she rushed forward reaching for my hand. Holding it, she curtsied lightly and pressed my fingers against her velvety lips. I pulled my hand away politely, noticing the ruby red mark she'd left behind.

"I am Sylvie, one of Prince Marston's mates. This lovely lady behind me." She turned and gestured to the other woman climbing down the stairs. "This is Kandrah, another mate to the Prince."

Kandrah reached the bottom and stepped close beside Sylvie. She took reached out for my hand and kissed it as she curtsied.

"High-mate, I have been in awe of the beauty of your kingdom. I have never seen the forest before." Her voice was barely a whisper. As she spoke, she turned her large brown eyes away, staring at the ground behind me.

What the fuck is this, I thought to Leadanah. Why are his other mates here?

Are you jealous already? She laughed at me.

Clearly, I am not, but this is extremely rude.

I looked up at Rathon, and could see he felt my sentiment. Typically, one does not parade their other mates before one of higher rank. With me being the new high-mate, I should never have to see any of his others. Much less have them paraded before me without prior warning.

So, this is how it will be, I thought.

I looked back at the two women hostile. Both were lovely, with an exotic sort of appearance. They were both in their full human forms. Sylvie was still grinning widely at me. She had small pointy teeth and a little nose. She looked like her therio must be something fragile. She was tall, with auburn hair piled atop her head. Some of it hung in like a halo surrounding her shoulders. She wore a simple, delicate silver tiara. Her sky-blue gown was still sliding off her shoulders as though the design's intent was to have her small breasts nearly slipping out. The dress, while floor length, split at a high point at the front, nearly exposing her femininity as she moved. It clung to her body and sparkled like water in the sunlight. I could make out tiny diamonds sewn into the fabric.

"I am pleased to meet you," I said. "Your hair is made of the sun. I do not believe I have ever seen its likeness."

"Oh lord, thank you, you're such a sweetie," she said.

"Lady Kandrah, I am also glad to meet you. Your gown is lovely," I said.

In truth, it was very average. She wore a slender empire waisted gown of pale gray. The neckline dropped tastefully between her generous breasts, where a long gold chain dangled between them. Her brown hair was not done up but brushed neatly and left to drift loosely around her shoulders. Although, she was beautiful, in a sharp way. Her cheek bones were high, and she possessed a quiet sternness to her large, slanted eyes. She reminded me of a hawk, but her apparent timidness threw me for a loop.

"Lady Andley, I hope your heart is high on this day." Her eyes darted, touching my own briefly, before fluttering away once more.

"Oh, Kandrah, her heart must simply be all over the place." Sylvie giggled, not unkindly.

The carriage door burst open and slammed against the outer wall with a jolt. I gasped in surprise. We all turned our eyes skyward. Framed in the doorway stood an imposing figure, lowering one foot deliberately. I heard a quiet scoff from Rathon and looked to him just in time to witness his eyes roll.

"Presenting Marston of house Arktos, Prince of Sandor," a herald cried aloud from the bottom of the staircase.

Sylvie beamed up at him as the Prince began his heavy descent to the forest floor with the rest of us.

I gazed at Rathon rather than the Prince, and saw hatred radiating from his face. A low growl rumbled up from beneath his chest. Sylvie and Kandra turned to watch the prince's approach, and did not notice Rathon's reaction.

As Marston came to the bottom step, Rathon willed a smile into his face and stamped down his enraged snarl.

"Rathon, king in the forest," the Prince boomed. "I rather expected a party to meet us. True, I brought a parade of entertainment for you and your nobles. The rest of the carriages are filled with delights."

"My prince, this is a joyous affair for you I'm sure, but for our people it is a somber day. Andley is well loved among her people. They mourn her departure."

"I am sorry to hear it, Rathon. I am certain you will bring home a new princess for your people soon."

"Was your journey restful, Marston?" asked Rathon, ignoring the jab.

"Yes yes, this part of the kingdom was always most pleasant to travel, back when I was a boy. I missed its tranquility. I don't believe I have been this way since your rebellion." He laughed. "I didn't see any starving people Rathon. I hope you have not exaggerated their plight."

"If the Prince wants to see how the peasantry live, I can accommodate this. The trouble lies further south. Much further from the capital," said Rathon bluntly.

"Oh no, jeez Rathon don't be so dour. The provisions from Sandor have followed. You do what you will with it all. I trust your soldiers are on the march home?"

"The troops left for Sandor this morning. You certainly passed them on the road? A thousand men."

"I saw no wolves among them." The Prince sniffed. "Surely you could have sent some of your elites."

"The wolves weren't part of the negotiations. The King thought it unwise to conscript pack animals," Rathon said. His voice was maddeningly calm despite the obvious taunt.

To call one a pack animal was to comment on their loyalty or stupidity. No one was fool enough to believe Rathon's wolves were stupid.

"Well, a shame, but I suppose I could not take all that you hold dear. The female is a small token in lieu of elite wolves, but I am certain she'll earn her price. A rare beauty I have heard!" Maston said this with a tone of friendly sarcasm, as though he could not sense the dangerous rage rising in

Rathon standing a mere foot away. The Prince turned his attention to me now.

"Look at me," he said softly.

His dark brown eyes forced themselves on me, willing mine to lock onto his gaze. They had an impression of boyish mischief. His face was hauntingly handsome. He had a hard, square jaw and sharp cheekbones. I noticed a sprinkle of freckles along his nose. He would have been very charming I thought, if he wasn't so imposing. He smiled at me, exposing two large canine teeth.

"Andley, you're as lovely as the rumors suggested. Surely Rathon couldn't trade his whole army to equal your value," he said quietly, as though his words were a secret between us.

Rathon's going to murder this man some day, I thought to Leadanah.

She grunted in agreement.

"A shame his need is so successful, I hear he is loath to let you go. My dear, don't believe you were traded cheap or easily."

Rathon stared into the sun. Resolute to maintain his calm.

"My prince," I said with a polite curtesy. "I am grateful for your assistance to my people. I go freely and hope to be the bridge between our kingdoms."

"Ah, yes. I suppose that's what these deals are really for at the end of all these meetings. A union to create alliances of blood between rival clans."

Marston spoke with an air of disinterest as he waved his hand.

"Luckily, we have lots of opportunities to create blood allies and so I get lots of lovely and rare mates from some of the most powerful houses. But none of my dear, are as rare as you or come from such a high seat."

He grinned and once again I found my hand being kissed. He glanced up at Rathon as he did this.

"Well, king in the forest, I hope you have said your goodbyes to your ward. Once your troops are integrated into Sandor's army, the march back will begin, and we will help open the pass. That should solve your little problem in a jiffy," he said, grinning.

Marston pulled me from Rathon's side, guiding me gently to the outstretched hands of Sylvie.

"A shame the war will be so short with the contract conditions being so, so long," Marston taunted.

I turned back at Rathon and saw the wretchedness in his eyes, although the calm hold he had over himself remained. I turned lightly away from Sylvie's hands and curtsied low before him, exposing my neck. When I rose, he cradled my hand and turned it palm up. He kissed the sensitive skin of my wrist, catching my startled eyes with his own ocean green gaze.

"Goodbye Andley." His voice as always held a sense of calm that moved through me like a stream. Always reliable, always knowing where to go.

"Rathon," I whispered.

Before I could say anything else, Marston turned away and began walking back to the carriage.

"Come on dear, don't drag it out," Sylvie whispered as she too curtsied. "King in the forest, I have been glad to meet you."

Kandrah followed Sylvie's example. "King in the forest, an honor."

"Come dear," Sylvie spoke into my ear, pulling me away gently. "Don't look back. You will hurt him."

I turned compliantly away from Rathon and heeded Sylvie. She stroked my hair as I walked up the staircase. I knew she meant to be kind, but the image of a rabbit being lovingly stroked before a knife is plunged into its neck came to mind.

"Darling is this a common hair color in the forest? It seems different each time I look! What do you call it?" Sylvie's tone was kindly and appeasing.

I entered the carriage and heard the heavy door close behind.

Chapter 4
Andley

"Leadanah?" I called to her, desperate. "Leadanah come forth, I need you. Leadanah? I stumbled around a vast darkness, seeking her. Every step felt like I would fall through the floor. I could hear cracking class as my toes sought a safe path through the pitch block around me. I inched forward only when the sound didn't come.

"Leadanah," I sobbed. Never had she failed to answer me before. I would take even her snapping teeth in the back of my mind, telling me to shut up.

A glow formed around me and the darkness retracted. Soon I could see the space before me and longed for the blessed darkness once more. There was nothing. Only empty space surrounding me. No ground, no sky, no wall or tree. Leadanah was nowhere in my sight. I wanted to move forward and look for her, but now that I could see there was no ground to walk upon; I was frozen in terror.

"Leadanah come back," I screamed into the nothingness.

My panic was setting in and I trembled, sinking to my knees, sobbing.

"Andley! Andley! Wake up."

I jerked forward from my sleeping body gasping as though I'd been underwater. I looked around the dim room frantically, not recognizing my surroundings at all.

Leadanah? I thought desperately.

Andley you were screaming what has happened? The soft, annoyed rumble of Leadanah's voice rolled through me.

"I had a nightmare," I said, rubbing my face with my palms. I was startled to find wet soft fur surrounding my cheeks.

"Oh!" I gasped. As I realized my wings were also outstretched, I had forced us into our dimidium form.

I've lost myself, I thought, feeling like a small child who found she has wet the bed.

Andley are you alright? I could not see your nightmare. Leadanah said. This was not uncommon. We do not always share our minds when we were both asleep.

I told Leadanah of my nightmare, how she was gone from me and there was no ground to walk on.

I am afraid, Leadanah. I have not known fear like this since my parents died. This long doom I feel coming.

Our parents, Andley, Leadanah finished after a time. I felt her remembering, snatching short glimpses, like sunlight peeking through a curtain. I felt a bit calmer.

Ours, I corrected myself. Was I really screaming?

"No, not outwardly, I don't think," said Leadanah.

"Andley, I know you are afraid. You need to keep your wits."

I breathed heavily, wrapping our wings around me. I stroked the soft feathers for comfort.

I looked around the wood paneled room lit by a dim oil lamp. I watched the crystal swaying gently around it. The silk slid along the fur and feathers on my body. It was so soft I thought I'd slip right off the bed if we hit a bump.

"Andley sweetie!" Sylvie called. "Do join me for tea. You have slept in so late. Breakfast is done."

"Don't come in! Wait! I called frantic as the curtain twitched open.

"Oh! Goodness!" she exclaimed.

I shrieked and pulled the comforter up high to cover myself, instinctively surrounding myself with my wings. There was a brief extension of quills and spikes before my shock receded. Leadanah howled with laughter as she receded, allowing me to take over.

"Sylvie, I wish you had knocked," I gasped.

"My lady I apologize." Sylvie turned away, retreating from my cabin.

64

I drew a shaky breath and returned to my human form.

"It's ok, Sylvie, you may enter. I am sorry I frightened you."

Sylvie peeked through the curtain, still looking embarrassed.

"My lady, forgive me. I didn't mean to react so rudely. I am sorry I was startled. I didn't expect…"

"I know my therio is a little startling. Most do not have feathers, quills and fur all at once," I said.

"And wings! Oh, they are magnificent."

"Ah yes. Wings."

"Andley, may I see? I promise I will not be startled," she pleaded.

"No," I said flatly. "I don't like people to see my therio."

Silvie leaned on the doorframe, crossing her arms below her breasts and tilting her head.

"I am, well Sylvie, I am a little greedy about it to be truthful," I admitted.

Sylvie smiled knowingly. "Well, you'd not be such a mystery if you flaunted yourself about like a common floozy. It's a good thing. The strongest women maintain an air of mystery I think," she said brightly.

I smiled, trying not to like her as she chatted on.

"Now you know what? it's a good thing I glanced you. I shall help to spread the gossip and increase your mystique." She winked.

"You have tea?" I asked.

"Yes, my lady. It is in the dining room."

"Is the Prince there?" I asked cautiously.

Sylvie frowned. "No, dear."

The tension left my shoulder blades slightly. I was doing my utmost to stay clear of him since our first encounter in the carriage.

"He is with Kandrah. He is unlikely to come out of his cabin," she said reassuringly.

I got up from the bed, spilling the silk sheets to the floor and pulled the simple traveling gown overtop my head. Tying the sash around my waist, I went with Sylvie. I had rather enjoyed her company the last two days, and her tea. She was so disarming; it felt as though I'd known her for years. I hated it.

As Silvie poured the tea, seductive muttering flowed from behind Marston's cabin door. His voice was low and smooth. If he'd been speaking a foreign language, the sound alone might light the flame of desire, but the words he spoke promised pain rather than pleasure.

I heard a soft whisper from Kandrah, and it was hard to know if it was from fear or glee. Might have been both for all I could know. Silvie chattered senselessly as the small sounds carried on behind the door. She was telling me about the court dramas and bedroom politicking, not that she really knew anything about that, she swore. When an intense pounding of wood on wood could not be ignored, and the low moaning of the Prince's voice was suddenly drowned out by a cry that was clearly painful.

"Oh dear, I had better go relieve her," Sylvie said with a sigh. "Don't be alarmed, sweety. This happens all the time; you may want to take your tea to your room though as I don't believe you are quite accustomed." Sylvie smiled brightly, holding her hands downward and fanning them toward me. "Go on, Andley. Shoo shoo."

She could not wholly hide the trepidation in her sparkling eyes. I gathered up my tea and turned away as she changed rapidly into a yellow and peach feathered therio and rose, marching resolutely into the Prince's room.

"Sylvie."

I heard the relief in Kandrah's voice as the door closed behind them.

I'd like to know what he's doing to them, Leadanah piped up. Sounds like it starts out okay.

I have a feeling that even if they enjoy it, he quickly ensures that they don't, I responded. He might have to actually try to kill you to end your glee though, I'd imagine.

Leadanah laughed as though she might like to see him try. I retreated to my own quarters and sipped my tea, chatting internally with Leadanah. While we were both equally conscious, my body transformed comfortably into dimidium. Times like these made me feel most at ease. Talking to Leadanah was like humming a perfect song. We knew all the words as they came up and saw each other's world as one. I wondered how anyone brings themselves to integrate their therio, how the void could ever be filled. I imagined integration to be much like killing half of yourself and then bending the corpse to move to your will like a necromancer.

Chapter 5

Leadanah

As Andley slept, I stretched out of her mind like a shadow creeping across the room as the sun fades from a window. Waking, I finally merged with the darkness surrounding us to mingle with the shadows cast by the blue light of the moon. As I rose, our body shifted into my form. I dropped to the floor and moved quietly on all fours, creeping to the curtained doorway listening for signs of the others. By the low rhythmic sway of their bodies, I could tell they were all asleep save for the slaves far away at the front of the carriage.

I crept through the doorway still holding myself low, my flat belly nearly dragging on the hardwood like a serpent. As I passed through, I used the clawed fingers on my wing to pull the curtain closed and then pulled myself in larger strides across the room. Still using my wings like spider's legs, carefully not leaving claw marks in the soft wooden panels, I pulled myself up the wall to the window and slipped through.

The night was crisp as the breeze hummed through the quills that hung down my back like hair. The small down feathers on my breast puffed out slightly as goosebumps rose, hardening my exposed nipples. Standing there drinking in the night, I raised my wings and let the air flow around them, using the force to hold me in place for a moment before finally allowing the air current to lift me away from the cumbersome earth.

With one strong downward pull, I rose higher than the trees looming on either side of the wide stone path. Using the canopy to cover myself, I flew ahead of the caravan. The stars were on full naked display tonight, yet the moon covered herself so only her sly smile could be seen. Her light gleamed along my ivory feathers as the cool wind streaked through the fur adorning my lower body.

I had felt so restless in the caravan; the endless rocking and creaking set my teeth on edge. I wasn't sure if I needed to hunt, fuck, or fly. Right now, I felt at peace, so I thought I would just glide on the currents tonight. I was nearly drowsing when I glanced down and saw the heat marks of small shapes lined at regular intervals throughout the trees, skirting the road. I dipped down lower to see what was giving off the heat signatures and was pleased to see they were wolves. Rathon's pack was steadily lining the path for miles ahead of the caravan. I looked back and saw several others moving swiftly from the back of the line, making their way to the head moving the pack forward one wolf at a time. Apparently, they intended to follow Andley the whole way to Sandor. I should have known Rathon would not let her go without holding on in some way or another. I imagined he was even now seeking a way into the castle itself.

I dove silently into the canopy and landed gently on a high tree branch above one of the sentries. Rathon's wolves were always on guard. I knew this one would pick up my scent in short order. I kept to the far side of the tree trunk and dug my claws in, tucking myself neatly behind it. I have always enjoyed watching them. Their controlled, calculating wildness always intrigued. They were so well trained, so disciplined they could maneuver together as one body; seemingly as though they were telepathic with each other.

I heard a low rumbling from the wolf below me as he crouched low to the ground. He had picked up my presence before my scent. The fur on the back of his neck rose and trailed in a hard line along his spine. I saw his ear tilt in my direction as he lifted his nose to the air. They always react this way when my presence becomes known to them. It is what makes me certain that I carry no trace of Andley while I am controlling our mind and body. The feeling toward me must be the closest to fear Rathon's brave wolves ever get. They know a predator when it stalks them.

I tried once to approach a young warrior on sentry, similar to how this wolf was now. I had taken up a spot in a tree, upwind from him. As he caught my scent, it was as though the air were filled with the aura of a lightning strike. He'd raised his face to the treetops, sniffing rapidly while his fur lifted like static along his back. He snarled and crouched low, ready to spring.

I had called out to him, saying I would do no harm, that I only wanted to meet him. I dropped to the earth, landing several feet in front of him, so he would not feel crowded or under attack. Before I could utter another word, the wolf was upon me, tearing at my throat. I have taken many lives, warriors, wild ones and those in between, for equally varying reasons. I have no qualms about that, but I would never seek to kill one of Rathon's wolves.

I dug my claws deep in between his ribs and crushed them with my hands. But still the wolf fought, straining to rip my throat out and end me alongside him. I kept squeezing his muscular body and ravaged him with the claws on my feet and wings, tearing him nearly to ribbons until he weakened and began shifting back into a man. He held my neck in his blunt teeth, still trying to kill me until the moment he finally died. Looking upon him, torn to shreds, it was the only time I felt bad about killing.

When they found the body of their fallen wolf, it caused such an intense ruckus across the forest. Not only was Rathon unafraid of the beast capable of what I'd done, he was furious. He sent his wolves out and like extensions of his own body they reached into the forest hunting with a rage so intense it was though they'd set fire to the villages. In his hunt for me, Rathon and his pack rooted out every wild therio who'd been camping in the forest or villages. They either tore them apart, or chased them back to the valley. Villagers who'd been harbouring them were banished, and the village mayors, disposed for incompetence or treason for allowing wild therios to reside in the forest. This went on for months. Andley was most distressed. She'd been forbidden from moving about the forest without a guard. Rathon's wrath had terrified her and horrified the nobles. Rathon never outwardly expressed his rage by yelling and thrashing things around like other men. No, he is silent while the storm gathers. His rage narrows into a singular point like the end of a spear. He plots, he drives, he hunts. Anything he tells his wolves to kill becomes a fleeing rabbit.

I had considered killing his pack when he sent them out, if not simply to convince him to hide rather than to hunt. Such a thing would have restricted me more, though. What was I going to do? Kill the whole pack? I thought of killing Rathon, which would have essentially solved my problem at the time. But I doubted Andley would be of much use if Rathon was suddenly violently murdered. It is also unfortunate that whatever Andley loves, I love too in some vague way.

Presently, I climbed to the top of the canopy and moved away from the pack. The others would be soon alerted to my presence.

"How boring," I groaned.

I knew I wouldn't be able to get closer than a mile to any of them now. I changed my trajectory to move deeper into the forest and picked up speed to get well ahead of the caravan and Rathon's pack. I hoped to be finished with my business by the time they caught up with me. The big ones typically make their dwelling where the forest is darkest. Hopefully, I could find a pretty one. I thought fondly of the ordeal to ensue and still couldn't decide if I wanted to fuck or fight. Maybe I'll get both. I grinned, beating my wings harder thrusting myself deeper into the forest.

The scent of a wild therio wafted through the canopy as I skimmed the treetops. A male's musk, thick with earth, raw meat and burned wood. I grasped the top of the tree and pulled myself downward headfirst along the tree, using my tail to aid me in a circular slithering movement around branches until I came to where the main branches and the trunk began. I watched him for a time move about his encampment.

He was tall and sleek in stature with the kind of muscles built by living in nature. His hair was trimmed short on the top and front of his head, but he allowed it to hang long down his back. Standing tall through the hair were sharp horns, which ran in single file from the top of his head and down his back and down a long whiplike tail. His face had high cheekbones with small scales protecting the outside edge of his brows. His nose extended into a small snout, but the lower half of his jaw held a sharp curve of a man's, much like a mask. His eyes had vertical slit pupils and were light green with golden flex like sunlight. The scales adorning his ribs and hips glittered in

71

shades of blue and green. For all the reptilian features, his form was mostly that of a man with only long talons on his extended toes and claws instead of fingernails.

He was starting a fire, apparently to prepare his evening meal.

Oh, dear, I thought amused.

Lying in a heap next to the fire pit was the body of what I could only assume was his companion. Cannibalism isn't as uncommon as the civilized would hope. In fact, on the fringes of society's veil, it is very common.

He placed a steel pot filled with water over the fire and added handfuls of chokecherries, wild mint, and a dash of chamomile to it. First tea, then his friend would be soup. He began chopping roots and potatoes. He put the food in a neat pile, then began the work of carving the body.

I watched with passive interest as he prepared his dinner while humming a doleful song in a deep baritone. He broke the bones and scraped out the marrow, sucking it off one clawed finger, saving only the two femurs for the soup stock. When he was finished, he gathered up the rest of the corpse and carried it into the trees, well enough away from his own camp.

The water had finally boiled when he returned. He poured some out into a pitcher carved out of wood, then placed the soup ingredients into the pot. Now finished with his preparations, he sat peacefully on a pile of logs arranged into a couch and leaned back, watching the fire.

He was so serene, sitting there with his back to the cold dark forest drinking fresh hot tea. I wondered what could have occurred between the two men to have led to one of them eating the other. There was no sign of starvation, no semblance even of a struggle. It was obvious that two men had been traveling together. There were two nests made up near the fire pit, and the belongings of two very different characters lay about.

He finished his tea in long gulp and dropped the pitcher to his side. He hung his head back, looking straight into the trees. From his angle, he could probably see a gap in the canopy and so was looking at the stars, his neck exposed, so easy to slide open. He let out a deep satisfied sigh and seemed to slump into the couch with one arm up around the backrest; his other shoulder dropped. Soon, I could see slight movement coming from that hidden shoulder. It rose slightly, slowly, in a rhythmic motion. I was pleased to realize he was jerking off. His head still hung relaxed and upward, his mouth a grinning slit, the points of his teeth sticking out slightly. He let out another small sigh that had a light, growling undertone. Not wanting to miss the show, I slithered back up the tree so I could move undetected between the treetops for a frontal view.

I propped myself silently in a tree just before the light of his fire and watched his abs flex as his hips started their small forward thrust into the movement of his hand. The slow, long caresses that if I let go on, would become a series of strong, sharp strokes. I watched his forearms flex with each upward movement as his thick, hard cock seemed to already be throbbing with cum.

Oh no, I couldn't let that happen. I slunk to the base of the tree pulling myself forward on the grass as I rose to my feet. I pulled the quills on my head back to hold them like hair down my back, and I dropped my wings down, wrapping them like a low skirt around my hips.

"Excuse me," I purred, smiling as politely as an angel.

He paused his stargazing, looking around curiously but unalarmed, only mildly surprised. His eyes fell on me, and he barred his teeth as though warning me. He left his arm around the back of the couch though, and the movement of his hand only slowed a little.

"Would you care to join me?" he asked, smiling. "I have some soup if you'd like to stay for dinner after."

"It smells very good. I may stay if there's time."

I walked forward through the light of his fire, and he started with surprise.

"Are those real wings?"

"Why yes, they are. Do you like them?"

"You fly?" he asked incredulously.

"Yes, how do you think I dropped in on you so?"

He never stopped his slow stroking as we talked. From this close, I could see how his cock generously filled his palm so that each of his clawed fingers barely met around it.

"May I?" I asked, grinning.

73

I sat down on his log couch beside him and leaned, placing my hand over his own, so we were stoking him together.

"Mmm, that's nice," he said, removing his hand and placing it behind his head.

I stroked his cock, feeling the texture of it in my hand, as he lifted his hips slightly with each deep stroke. I stopped abruptly and removed my hand to watch it throb.

"Why'd you stop?"

"Felt like stopping." I laughed. "Think I'll leave."

I pretended to get up, and he grabbed my wrist.

"This your little game?" he asked.

He pulled my hand back and forced it to recommence the motion on his cock. "Your game is a lot like my game."

He reached forward with his free hand and ran his clawed fingers through my quills. They made a sound like rain on leaves as they moved against each other.

"These are nice," he said. "You look dangerous."

He placed his hand around my throat and calmly started squeezing.

I smiled.

"Stop," I said.

He kept working my hand up and down squeezing his own tight over mine. My nipples rose with my fur, and heat radiated from below.

"You don't seem to mind," he cooed, releasing my hand so I could keep up the rhythm on my own. He reached forward and pressed his clawed fingers into me, thrusting deep. "You don't seem to mind at all."

His hand gripped my throat tighter, and I felt my pussy clench with excitement. I dug my claws between the delicate scales on the back of his hand, drawing blood. He released my throat, and I snatched his hand back, forcing his fingers in between my teeth and bit down, also drawing blood.

He ripped his fingers from between my legs with a cry of pain and, seizing my waist, he threw me to the ground. I landed on my ass in the dirt and then laughed, recovering quickly from the unceremonious handling. I leaned back on my elbows, exposing my breasts invitingly.

"Oh, you want get fucked like that do you?" he asked, shaking his hand rapidly as though trying to fling the pain away. "That fucken hurt," he said, sucking his wounded fingers.

I grinned wickedly up at him as he bore down on me.

As he sank his cock into me, he also sank his teeth into my shoulder, breaking the small delicate feathers penetrating my skin. I gasped with pain and clawed his back. I found that the scales there were thicker and overlapped in a solid plating of armor. So, I grabbed the spiked horn on the back of his head and pulled, forcing him to release my shoulder. The wound began healing, but the feathers would take forever to molt and regrow.

Next, he placed his sharp mouth around my breast and bit down with surprising lightness and began flicking his tongue around my nipple. I let go of his back and ran my hands through my quills, pulling on them in distracted pleasure. I felt his claws raking my skin, drawing hot wet blood to stain my fur and feathers. He plunged into me ruthlessly, without tiring, until I felt the pressure rising inside me. With each push forward, he struck the little spot that is so rarely found. It seemed to spark like a jolt of electricity each time. With every jolt, I was closer to the surge of orgasm.

He stopped, pulling his long dick out slowly while I tried to use my legs to press him forward and back in.

He reached down and grabbed me by the throat once again and lifted me up to drag me toward the tree line. Slightly alarmed, I clawed the back of his hand again, but he did not flinch. I wondered briefly if this idiot thought he could kill me. Maybe that's why his friend was dead. Likes to finish with a kill.

"You're here to get fucked, aren't you?" he asked maliciously.

He slammed me against a tree, and I felt a twinge of actual anger as my head slammed into the trunk. Before I could rub my throbbing head, he pulled me forward by the base of my quills, holding me up on my knees.

"Oh my god, yes!" I cried out and began to laugh.

As I opened my mouth, he jammed two fingers into it, gagging me. He drew back and forth, sliding his fingers in and out of my throat. I relaxed my jaw as he held me there, holding me up by my quills, fingering my throat.

75

Holy fuck, I thought, wide-eyed.

He pushed me forward, so I had to catch myself before my face hit the ground and pulled my face roughly forward to his cock.

"What do you think? Are you my slave?"

I looked up at him, genuinely shocked at his audacity. He must be mad, I thought. But I felt my watering mouth yawning open for him, and he forced his cock downward in my throat. He held my head and hips as he drove himself in and out. As more saliva was forced out of my mouth, it ran down onto my breasts. He grabbed one in a rough clawed hand and held the back of my head still with the other. His movements became short and sharp; I could feel his whole cock throbbing with each grunting thrust.

My pussy clenched with want as my clit pulsated, as though jealous of the attention my throat was getting. I reached up, holding his hips and gleefully felt the hard flexing in his abdomen. I pressed him back and dragged in a quick breath before his firm hand pushed me down on him again. His grunts turned into moaning; the sound escaped him with each heavy cycle of his thrusts.

I thought of how his cock might feel throbbing in my throat as he came, and I reached down between my legs. I was starting to get lightheaded; I thought I would have to stop him in a second before I actually passed out. I rubbed my clit feverishly and slid my own fingers into myself. I was already so close.

I will have to find this man again, I thought.

With perfect timing, he pulled his cock from my throat; it was dripping wet. I took a deep gasp of air.

He grabbed me by my chin; his claws dug into either side of my cheeks and lower jaw he squeezed, forcing my mouth to remain open.

"Look at me," he commanded.

I looked up, still panting for air, and our eyes locked and we recognized the savage evil in each other.

"I'll kill you if you do that again," I said.

He grabbed my arm roughly and flipped me over.

"I think you could," he said, pressing me down with his hand between my wings. I allowed my breasts and face to be pressed into the grass. His claws lingered as he lifted his hand back and caressed the soft feathers on my wings. This surprised me. Most of the time, men are afraid to touch them.

I cried out at the sudden violence of his cock as he pounded me with brutal disregard for my pleasure. My pussy dripped with ecstasy and tightened around him, eliciting a pleased moan from him. I reached up and dragged my claws into the bark of the tree in front of me while bracing myself into the earth with the talons on my feet, raking trenches in the dirt, pushing back into him with each thrust. His strokes became faster, more resolute. A sharp moaning gasp escaped me with each breath.

"Fuck!" he groaned.

He grabbed my hips, pressing himself so deep in me that it would have hurt if I had not been in the throws of my own orgasm. I felt his cum shoot into me with each twitch of his cock. He pulled me down, finally ceasing his thrusts, so that I was sitting on his cock now still feeling him pulsating into me. He dug his claws into the tops of my breast penetrating me, while his cum slid down between my thighs.

I dropped my head back onto his shoulder and rocked lightly back and forth on his still-hard cock. He turned my head to the side and grazed his teeth tenderly along the side, feeling my pulse with his lips. We sat together, letting our racing hearts and breath come down before he gently pushed me forward, lifting me up so he could pull himself out.

I rose to my feet while examining the work I'd done on the tree. I grinned and followed him back to the fire pit. He tossed me a rag and gasped simultaneously as he saw his stew was boiling over.

"Shit, I hope it's not burned. I hate burned soup," he growled.

He pulled the pot out of the fire with his bare hands and placed it on the ground. Grabbing his ladle, he stirred and scooped up some soup. He tasted it and smiled.

"No, it's fine. Here, try," he said, offering me the ladle.

"Mmm, that's really good. Why'd you wanna eat your friend?" I asked. "You just knew he'd be tasty?"

"He was tasty, but also very annoying, and I do enjoy killing when I cum. It was just time."

"Come on, I hope he actually did something."

"Killed a little kid. Said he'd found one wandering too far from its village. He didn't have a reason, just wanted to," he said with disgust.

"That a line for you then?" I asked, laughing.

"It's not funny. Killing kids? I had a kid before I left home."

"Well, now he's dinner." I laughed.

He brought two bowls over, filled one and handed it to me. We ate silently, watching the fire.

"Do you know Dante of the star tribe?" I asked suddenly.

"I know Dante. He killed a mad therio a few nights ago." He stirred his soup slowly as he spoke.

"I heard. Were you at the gathering?" I sipped more soup.

"I was, but did not see the fight."

"Do you know what became of the boy, Isor?"

"Sad business," he began. My breath caught. "The shaman was ready to help him destroy his human, but the boy did not want to do it. So of course, the shaman and his parents were going to do it, but the boy fled. He hasn't been seen since. A child that young can't survive on his own."

I couldn't help the smile forming on my lips. "Perhaps he will find one of the towns, and someone will take him in."

"Maybe, but they will make his human integrate him. Either way, he is doomed. Some folks are looking for him. Dante is one. I feel for the parents."

I wondered why Dante would seek him out himself.

"And where are you traveling to? Are you also helping to find the boy?"

"No. I and my delicious companion," he gestured at his soup, "have been traveling together to deliver a message to Sandor from Brath and the therio chiefs." He placed the empty bowl on the ground beside his foot.

"What message would the wild therio tribes have for Sandor?"

He looked at me through slitted eyes. "I thought you were at the gathering?"

"I was there, but the fight broke out. I left after."

"It's not a message for everyone who is curious." He shrugged.

I frowned, making up my mind in a moment. A message from Brath, delivered by a therio to Sandor. After some gathering and pointless meetings. Disdain for Rathon's rule. I didn't need details.

I stood up and stepped swiftly in front of the man. He looked up at me, mouth slightly agape, eyes wide with confusion. I raised one clawed hand and slashed it through the air, slicing open his throat like a scythe through grass.

He gurgled, trying to scream groping wildly at the wound. He rose to his feet and tried to run. I grabbed him by the shoulders and drug him back to face me. His blood-covered hands stopped flailing at his throat and tried to push me away. I pulled him close, pressing the back of his head down, forcing his flesh onto my teeth. His wet screams rose, cracking uselessly in the night air.

When he stopped struggling, I lowered the body back down onto the logs. It slumped onto its side while the legs hung awkwardly over the side. Blood finished pouring from his neck, covering the lush moss. I wandered toward the fire where his belongings lay neatly packed on his nest. I opened the satchels and riffled through each pocket until I found a sheet of paper inside a flat leather pouch. Opening the fold, I read a short message scrolled up on the white parchment.

"Our neighbors in the valley have accepted your gracious invitation to feast."

I frowned. That wasn't much to go on. Maybe I shouldn't have killed him so soon. I glanced over to the dead male. His mouth had dropped open, and his eyes stared glazed and half open into the fire.

"Reptiles can be hard to kill," I mumbled to myself. "I had better make sure."

I was pretty sure he was dead, but couldn't risk him regenerating and still making it to Sandor. The missing message wouldn't change much, but it may buy Rathon time. Reaching down I grasped the base of his head at the space between his skull and spine. Bracing the body down with my foot, I pressed my claws between the scales and dug deep into his flesh. Squeezing the fingers of my other hand into the wound, I ripped the back of his neck open and slashed at the muscles and bone, severing the tendons, and pulled. His head flopped forward, but no blood spurted from the gaping hole.

"Must have been dead then," I said to myself.

I rose slowly into the air, lost in idle thoughts about Dante and his meetings. What could the wild therios possibly think Sandor or Brath would do for them? They couldn't really think they'd grant them the valley. Free rein in the forest, maybe? Stupid.

I landed next to a shallow pond to wash myself.

Dante couldn't have been involved in an attempt to overthrow Rathon. Despite their whining, life had been better for them since his rule began. I wiped the blood from my feathers absentmindedly, pondering the meaning of the message. When I'd finished, I rose listlessly to find the cart tracks.

I found myself suddenly approaching the entourage of carriages. All was quiet except for the occasional chatter of the guards strolling the length of the parade as it sat silently upon the tracks. I landed on the roof of the Prince's caravan and found the window to my compartment. I slid headfirst into the window and walked to mine and Andley's room to sleep.

Chapter 6
Andley

Rosy sunlight glowed on the panels all around me, igniting them with a soft heat that brought out the scent of cedar. Lying for a moment encompassed in a pile of silk pillows and a down-filled blanket, I watched tiny dust particles floating like fairies in a strip of light suspended across my body. Leadanah purred sleepily from within me, dream images of our mother slipping from her mind as she slowly woke. I ran my hand along the wall beside me, feeling the new heat of the day, then rose to dress and join Sylvie and Kandrah for breakfast.

When I didn't find them in the main cabin, I searched Sylvie's room but still did not find them until I heard soft crying coming from Kandrah's cabin and paused listening at the heavy curtain.

"Hold on, sweetie," Sylvie's voice slipped through.

She was talking in a calming tone, as though speaking to a child, but I could hear a slight shake in her voice like the nervous twittering of a bird. I felt Leadanah listening in. Kandrah gasped and then cried in despair.

"God, Sylvie," she sputtered. "I want to go home."

"Kandrah, you mustn't talk like this. It's not so bad. We will be back in the castle soon, dear. You, you can write home."

"He's going to kill me if he keeps this up," Kandrah moaned.

"We will be home soon. He will give you a break. See the other girls. I'll, I'll talk to him, Kandrah. I'll ask him to leave you be for a while," Sylvie purred.

"No, you must not tell him. Don't talk to him for me! He will get angry. You know he will! Please don't, Sylvie," Kandrah pleaded.

"I just don't know why he wants to be so rough with you. Darling, you really must try not to show distress. You know it only gets him excited."

"I, I can't, Sylvie, it hurts so bad. And he scares me."

"When it hurts and you must cry out; try to make it a sound like pleasure, dear. And don't look so frightened. You must learn to control your expressions. You can practice making pleasure faces in the mirror. It may seem silly, but no one will know. It has worked for me when he gets too rough."

"I can't, Sylvie. I'm not like you. I'm so small he could crush me with one hand. I wish I were dead. I don't know how much of this I can take."

"Stop that ridiculous talk right now, Kandrah! We will be home soon. Just make yourself scarce. He will forget about you for a while. Just stay here in your cabin for the rest of the trip. I will bring you your food and tend to your wounds."

I could hear Kandrah crying softly now. I imagined her thrown forward into her pillows, muffling her sobs.

"Stay in your room, honey. Out of sight, out of mind. You'll see. I'll keep him company."

Kandrah groaned, "Noooo." Her sobs became more desperate.

"Enough silliness. He doesn't hurt me the same way, and he likes my jokes. I'm okay. Stay in here. I will take care of you," Sylvie said.

Kandrah's muffled sobs grew louder for a moment as Sylvie swung the curtain to the side, stepping out of the cabin. She looked up at me, startled.

"Oh, Andley, I didn't know you were up," she said cheerfully.

Her eyes met mine, and we saw each other's terror.

"Pay Kandrah no heed. She will be okay. You don't have to worry about yourself, sweetheart. He doesn't … what I mean, dear, is your status will protect you. You will be head mate to the Prince. He cannot harm you. Okay? Please don't be frightened."

Her voice raced, yet she still sounded like she was singing.

I stared at her. My eyes must have been swimming with fear.

"No, really, Andley. Kandrah is new. She hasn't learned yet; that's all. She will be okay. We all learn how to handle Prince Marston in our own way. She will find hers."

"What does he do to her?" I asked, trembling.

What indeed, Leadanah thought darkly.

Silvie drew in a deep breath and let it out in a quiet huff. Her shoulders were drawn up as her eyebrows knitted together.

"That is not talk for ladies or friends to share amongst each other, Andley. Please don't ask anyone about what the Prince does with them," she said sternly. "We must not gossip or pity ourselves or each other. Never ask your sisters about what may shame them." She softened her tone. "I know you don't understand love. It's okay. I am sorry I spoke harshly to you. I forgot for a moment where you are from. How you must have been loved."

I stared confused, while Leadanah barked about the Sylvie's audacity in the back of my mind.

"Rathon looks to be gentle," she said sweetly.

"What?" I asked. Startled away from thoughts of Kandrah. "What do you mean?"

"Don't worry, sweetheart, it isn't so obvious. The others don't have the same keen sense of smell as I do. It wasn't the sex, but the pheromones. I can smell them. You two were upset. But not to worry, it is a rare trait."

"I-It's, not," I stammered. "It's not wrong. Rathon and I are not related. We never saw each other the way others describe us. As siblings or him as a father to me. It's just how things turned out for us."

"Darling, of course not. Families change in war. We end up where we end up, if we live at all," Sylvie said, smiling.

She's distracting you, Leadanah said slowly. She wanted you to stop asking questions, so she's putting you out so you will think about other things.

It's working, I thought. How can she smell different kinds of pheromones? So distinctive? Like smelling the feelings of others?

That's a dangerous gift, Leadanah muttered darkly. It could get her killed.

"I need to bring poor Kandrah some tea, and then ready myself for when the Prince wakes. He may want to take a walk today or go riding. Would you like to come?" she asked.

A cloud must have moved away from the sun as she smiled, because the room shimmered and grew brighter as a beam of sunlight crossed over my eyes. I had to blink several times to adjust my eyesight.

I don't trust her, Leadanah growled.

"No thank you, Sylvie. May I join you over breakfast, though?" I asked.

"Yes, dear. Meet me in an hour." She patted my shoulder lightly as she passed.

We should get rid of her, Leadanah said.

What! no!

Too many people know our secret. She is one too many on our enemy's side. We need to get rid of her.

Leadanah! I'm shocked. We can't go around killing people because we are afraid of them. Don't talk like that, I countered.

Andley, you can't stop me if I decide to do something, Leadanah growled.

I forbid you from using this body we share to hurt her or anyone! I shall never speak to you again if you hurt her. She won't tell. She doesn't know, anyway.

Leadanah left such a silence that I began to squirm.

For the love we have and the body we share, I won't hurt her. Unless she becomes a real threat, she said resolutely.

I knew the argument was over just as I knew she would honor her promise.

I want to see the other one, Leadanah said. I want to see what he did.

I thought about arguing against it for a moment, but I was also curious. I wanted to know what this man was capable of.

I let Leadanah through so we could both look and then drew the curtain back slightly.

Kandrah was lying naked on her back with her eyes closed. She seemed to have passed out. Tears had pooled in the well of her eyes and spilled down the side of her face, soaking her hair. I could see why she lay exposed as she

84

was. To have anything touch her bruised and ripped body would be unbearable. Black markings ringed her throat and spread up to her chin and down her chest. Red and blue bite marks covered her breasts. There was dried blood forming a scab in streaks along her ribcage. My breath caught as I took in the injuries. Leadanah was eerily silent as she studied the scene.

Like a cat with a little mouse. The more she struggled, the more he hurt her, she whispered.

Are there men like this in the world? I asked Leadanah.

Many, she said, her tone final.

I let the curtain drop back into place, covering Kandra from view, and we began walking back to our room.

How do you know this? Have you met them before? I asked. How have you come to meet men like this?

I meet many men. Some are like this. They like how big their hands look holding something small. Some still, like how it feels when something fragile breaks in those hands, Leadanah explained.

Has this happened to you? I gasped inwardly.

Leadanah barked a short laugh. No.

What? How do you escape when one wants to hurt you? I asked.

Leadanah's chuckle was icy.

Andley, it is they who cannot escape.

My back shivered, like bugs were crawling down it. I looked at my hands, my heart racing.

Sylvie is right, Andley. Marston won't hurt us like that. Don't be afraid, Leadanah said as she retreated.

I stared at my hands in wonder. Leadanah has said our body is a weapon before, but she only meant that we have claws and teeth. We have wings, and it gives us an advantage. But a weapon? Capable of killing? A body that could fight a man like Marston?

I cringed as I thought of committing my own hands to the force of violence needed to kill. Suddenly, like turning on a light, I realized I had no idea where they'd ever been or what they'd done when I was not aware.

Does Leadanah kill with our body? I wondered privately.

A wave of dread and sorrow surged through me. I imagined Marston's hands around poor Kendrah's body, squeezing and tearing until she could only squeak like a mouse.

Has Rathon done these things? The question came to me like a shock.

I remembered his hands in my hair. Every bit as strong as Marston's. I'd seen Rathon fight. I knew he killed people; he's a warrior. I'd seen him sparring with the little boys in training. Holding flowers. Baring his claws. Building homes for our people. He once threw a man against a wall when he had insulted his father.

Andley, I need to tell you something. Leadanah's voice interrupted my private thought. Last night, I met a wild therio. He was carrying a message from Brath to Sandor. The note is in our room.

Leadanah explained how she had met a wild therio and discovered the note. There seemed to be holes in her story as she told it. She stole the note somehow and took off before he could stop her. She also explained for the first time that the wild therio had organized meetings that seemed to allude to a partnership with Brath.

We had always been aware that the wild ones gather from time to time and had some rudimentary kind of society. But I hadn't imagined they were organized or envisioned them to have any kind of culture. The story about the mad therio Justin surprised me, especially when Leadanah talked about a funeral ceremony. But the boy Isor, that both frightened and enraged me.

What if the messenger still comes to Sandor, though," I said out loud, forgetting myself in my distress.

He won't, Andley.

How do you know that? I asked.

I convinced him, for now, she said with a tone of finality.

I walked back to my room to find the note. Upon reading it, a stone settled in my stomach.

I have to warn Rathon somehow and try to find out more.

I know. We will have to wait and watch, she said. Act as though you know nothing for now.

I paced my room, holding the note, trying desperately to calm down. I had so many questions. Not just about the note, but everything I had just learned about the wild therios.

They have tribes? I asked.

They have everything the humans have, Andley. Has it never crossed your mind? Leadanah's voice was dry and bored.

No, I had no idea.

I suspect the wild ones don't cross the minds of anyone in the forest, except to hate and fear them. Perhaps a bit more thought would have stopped this.

My pacing ceased as I took in her meaning. Maybe it is not too late. We can talk to them.

Leadanah laughed. Who will talk to them?

You. Obviously.

Leadanah laughed again. No.

Well, Rathon can send an ambassador.

I don't think it would work, Andley. But before we can think about what to do, we have to find out more, and warn Rathon somehow.

"Lady Andley, are we still having breakfast together?" Silvie mercifully remained outside my room this time. I hid the note in my bodice and called out.

"Yes, Silvie, I will be there shortly."

I stood in front of the mirror and adjusted my hair, which had become disheveled as I'd rung it nervously between my fingers.

Breakfast with Sylvie was sweet and sunny. She was fully animated while chatting excitedly about her plan to go riding with the Prince. He entered the dining cabin and asked after Kandrah.

"Oh darling, you really tired her out. Let's let her rest. Besides, I'd like you to myself while I have the chance." She didn't skip a beat.

Marston scratched his cheek absentmindedly. His eyes wandered around the room and flitted to me briefly. I had noticed his face flushing every time he saw me. It wasn't a shyness. His face would contort briefly into a nearly imperceptible snarl.

"I suppose I was a little rough on her." He yawned. "Are you ready to go?"

Sylvie stood up, her food half eaten, and held her hand out to him. He reached for her and wrapped her into himself gently. They chattered on the way out, and I was left to spend the day in silent solitude.

The next day I saw Sylvie coming from Kandrah's room, a shadow cast across her face.

"How is Kandrah?" I asked as we passed each other in the corridor.

"She's..." Sylvie's face crumpled into itself for a moment. "She's very unwell."

Hours later, I met Sylvie again in the main cabin for dinner. She sat staring pensively out the window; she wore a yellow dress and had her auburn hair flowing loosely down her back. The sun once again lit up her hair like a halo.

"How is Kandrah?" I asked again.

Silvie turned from the window. I was shocked to see how her usually plump, smiling cheeks sagged, as though being dragged down by the grimace of her mouth. As she spoke, Prince Marston entered the room and seated himself at the table farthest from us. She rearranged her face into a passive stare as smoothly as sliding on a mask. I could still be the fear and pain shining from beneath it.

"Well, I'm afraid she's passed on," she whispered.

"Her injuries killed her?" I asked shocked.

"No, dear, injuries of the heart and mind—" Her words broke off, and she turned away sharply, facing the window once again.

Marston held his cup out for a servant to pour his wine. He glared at Sylvie, his face a promise of fury, as though daring her to go on.

"Please sit with me, Andley," she said. "We will be home soon. You should come with me to the front of the caravan to see the city. I am sure you've never seen anything like..." her voice cracked and she paused.

"Anything like it," she finished her eyes glittering with the swell of held-back tears.

Sylvie was right. I had seen nothing like this before. Although I don't think it had the effect on me she expected. A high wall stretched across the landscape, circling the buildings within. Many high towers rose like knives stabbing the sky. Smaller squat buildings surrounded them. In the very center, the castle loomed oppressively over the city. While all the other buildings were plainly made, with gray stones or wood planks, the castle walls were made with small white stones that glittered in the light. The setting sun glinted off the glass set in windows spattered throughout the castle spires.

I looked over at Sylvie as she stared with a faint smile at the rising city, the sun once again making love to her, playing on her skin deepening the blush of her cheeks and setting her hair alight. Despite everything, she appeared genuinely happy as though she, not I, was seeing the city for the first time in her life.

How does someone live the way she does and still look so happy? How can she smile in the setting sun when her friend is dead? I wondered.

Leadanah said, What would happen if she let the darkness touch her, Andley? Perhaps she is a bit mad. She must be.

I had such a nice life, I thought to myself. The city crept closer, coming to take it all away from me. A flare of rage rose in me, and I found myself angry with Rathon.

He sold me.

The thought seemed so distant from my own mind. The words carried my rage like a cold wind signaling the promise of a storm. I had been holding it back for so long.

Leadanah stop, I glowered angrily at her.

What? Don't blame me; that's all you. She tutted.

He didn't have a choice, I responded, seeking reassurance. The sunlight pierced my eyes, making them sting.

Andley, if you want my opinion, you can have it. No, I don't believe he had a choice. Prince Marston demanded you as a mate to spite him. He'd rather kill the man and be done with the whole thing. But still, selling people? Hard to say war wasn't more humane, she mused. Should one suffer so many can have peace? Should many die so one can live? Should your people die to keep their virtue? At the right price, are all people for sale? Those are the questions you should ask Andley. Not, is Rathon good or bad? He is neither. He is a man.

I didn't think you had given this so much thought, Leadanah, I said.

Nothing has ever happened to us to require so much of it. We have never been sold before, she responded cooly. I am not sure which is most evil, to be the seller or the purchaser of a person.

Chapter 7
Andley

As we approached the castle gates, a delegation on horseback from the King's guard met us. Extravagant bluing and etchings decorated each rider's armour, creating flowing patterns in the hard steel. Each was painted in rich hues, creating a rainbow of glittering steel. My heart quickened when I noticed soldiers were riding n their full therio forms beneath the bright colors and silks. Each was heavily armed glaring into the crowd with sharp intensity. The prancing step of hooves on cobblestone brought a clamour of ringing steel. The sun pierced through the shadows as edges of barding glinted mcnacingly, like hidden daggers from beneath the brightly coloured ribbons and sashes adorning the horses' massive bodies.

I wondered why they needed this much protection? Did their own citizens hate them enough to attack them? Did they fear attack from an enemy hiding in their own city? In the forest, Rathon and all the nobles walked freely with no fear of molestation.

But for how much longer will that be? Leadanah interrupted my thoughts. The noblemen fear the people because the people are desperate. Look at how skinny they are, while the rich want for nothing.

I shuddered, thinking of the reports of starvation in the hinterlands of the forest, while in the capital we had felt nothing of this.

Our carriage drove in the center of the wide street with the mounted soldiers surrounding us heavily. They waved heavy, armored hands to the crowds, smiling with pointed teeth at the curious people who'd gathered to watch the parade.

"Why are guards so heavily armed in the city?" I asked Silvie.

She looked confused. "Are they? I have never noticed." She peered out her window at one man striding beside us.

"Their ridiculous costumes conceal their armor and weapons. How clever."

She smiled knowingly at me. I smiled sweetly back at her, noting her apparent ignorance. I wondered if it was just her or if it was a privilege of all with a high station in the city not to notice such things. Although, it is possible she was being coy.

When I'd imagined the city, I had envisioned something closer to grass huts and logs. But I could not have been further from the mark. Except for the towers, which were richly built with stone and glass, the buildings that served as homes were made of mud or rotting wood planks. As we passed, I watched the people pause in their work and conversation to glare, sneering at the carts and caravans passing them. One woman stood watching the procession, her clothes worn to near threads. She was pressing a dead cat to her mouth, tearing its flesh away as bright red blood smeared her lips and poured from the creature, splashing onto her bare feet. Chewing on the meat, she raised the carcass up and held it back behind her head, then flung it with all her might at the caravan. It struck the wall beside my window.

"What on earth!" I gasped.

Before she could drop her arm back down, the guards set upon her, throwing her to the ground and kicking her in the ribs.

"Best to keep your head inside until we get closer to the city center, Andley. Don't worry, it is not like this all over." Silvie leaned over me and drew the shutter down over the window. As we continued down the road, the houses became sturdier; made of fresh wood and stone. The people, while still thin, had a healthier appearance. Their clothes had fewer patches, and the children all donned shoes of varying quality.

People came out of their homes and watched us pass. Children waved and Sylvie gleefully called back, throwing out candies to them. Most people seemed genuinely pleased to see the procession. There were, however, still some sour faces sprinkled throughout the fanfare. Those whose grim smiles seemed more like a snarl. Men crossed their arms over barrel chests, the fur on their arms rising. Many of these men called out, "Long live the King" or "God grant immortality to the King."

"What does it mean, Sylvie? They look so angry."

"Oh, dear, don't worry about the peasantry. They've really got no teeth. Besides, it is right that they love their king."

"Sylvie, no one looks like that when proclaiming their love for a king," I retorted.

She pressed her lips tight and took a short breath inward. "Some do not love the Prince. That's all. They want their good king to live forever."

"Nothing more?" I asked doubtfully.

Sylvie looked forward, watching the castle as we approached. She raised one eyebrow and frowned. The expression was so short that if I had not already been looking at her, I would have missed it. For in an instant, she plastered a bright smile upon her lips and ensured it met her sparkling eyes.

"Andley, see the castle? It glitters at this time of day. It is made of a beautiful stone called goshenite. It took decades to complete hundreds of years ago. Isn't it remarkable?"

The castle seemed to rise from the earth like a collection of spears tearing the sky. Indeed, it glittered and sparkled as the sun danced upon it. The ever-changing shift of light glinting across its face mesmerized me.

"I wish we'd come at sunset. It is magical to see then," Sylvie said. "Come, Andley, it's time to get dressed."

Sylvie led me to the dressing room in the rear cabin where servants had prepared wet hot towels for us to wash with. They had laid out clean gowns for each of us, and I noticed there was a third gown laid next to Sylvie's. She halted when she saw it and marched to the back entry. I could nearly feel rage flying from her as she opened the door, but she spoke slowly and calmly into the room beyond.

"There has been a third gown laid out. I expect someone has made a mistake. There are two ladies to dress. Do come remove it this instant. I do not expect anyone intended to wound with their carelessness. But it has indeed wounded me."

Another angry voice sounded from within the servant squatter. "Idiot girl! The lady Kandra is dead. Why would you lay a dress out for her?"

There was a loud clatter and a painful cry moments before a young woman scuttled into the dressing room with her head down, muttering apologies, calling herself an idiot and saying she hadn't known. Sylvie watched her move across the room and snatch up the gown.

"Carelessness is equal to cruelty," she said, her face red.

The young woman left bowing and crying with apologies. Sylvie didn't look at her as she closed the door quietly behind her. I thought to myself that this must be the closest to yelling and door slamming Sylvie gets.

"I will give you privacy, Andley, and dress in my room. I washed this morning. Just pop this door open. If you require assistance, the girls will come."

I watched her silently as she glided past me, picked up her own gown and was gone. The gown left out for me was more of a contraption than clothing. It consisted of a satin material which wrapped precariously around my breasts and waist, spiraling down one leg. The wrap ended in a tapered strap around my ankle. The top layer was a thin intricate gold lace, which was carefully clipped to the edges of the wrap. The skirt hung loosely about my calves. Looking in the mirror, I was mildly horrified to see that the wrap barely covered my private parts, and my breasts threatened to slide out from beneath the soft material.

Does everyone get to see me naked next? I wondered aghast. As I moved, the wrap threatened to ride up, exposing me on both sides. At that moment, another servant returned to the room.

"How is this worn without it sliding right off?" I asked her.

The servant said, "My lady, it will not move. You may walk normally."

"How?" I exclaimed, exasperated.

"My lady, the material grips your skin as you move. It will tighten and hold when you walk."

I squinted at her and cautiously moved my body around. Daring the wrap to slide. Sure enough, I could feel it grip my skin and tighten around me with every movement as though it were alive. I raised my arms into the air rapidly and felt the wrap grip my breasts tightly. The servant giggled.

"You see, my lady? You are quite safe."

I starred at the remarkable thing on my body and began examining it.

"What is it?" I asked.

"My lady it is a dress," the servant said confused.

"No, the material. What is it made of?"

"Oh, lady I am sure someone knows, but I do not. The other girls think wizards make it."

"Wizards," I repeated bluntly.

"This is what the girls say. I have never seen a wizard, so I do not know if they are real," she said.

She stared at me expectantly. My hair and makeup were complete. She had painted intricate wings beside my eyes and temples and sprinkled a shining cover upon my exposed skin. My hair was piled in a high braid secured from the top of my forehead to the back of my neck. It hung loosely from the nape of my neck and down my back. She had woven gemstones throughout the braid and clipped still more in the loose hair down my back.

"Yes, thank you that is all," I said.

I felt the carriage stop at that moment and heard Sylvie call from the door for me to come to her. I came out and saw she wore a simple, pale gold gown. In her hair, she had woven colorful gemstones, much like my own. Her makeup was plain. She smiled at me and couldn't fully hide her sorrow. This frightened me a little bit.

"Andley, I hope the journey away was mostly enjoyable for you. I know there was some unpleasantness. I want you to know that I am here, always. I will show you the concubine quarters when I get the chance, and you are always welcome with us. It is not improper for the high-mate to be seen with the others. It is up to you." She reached for my hands and held them both. "I haven't yet told you about Anabelle. She is the Prince's, well she's not high-mate anymore. She has his children however, and I, I implore you not to interfere with her. Anabelle is not a bad person. She has children to protect. She takes much of the Prince's attention. I expect this won't bother you."

The sound of heavy footsteps lumbered toward us. "The price cannot hurt you. Remember that."

"Remember Rathon, remember your home when you are afraid." She placed a cool hand on my cheek. "I am sorry, Andley. I hope you will be well."

The Prince entered the room and approached from behind Sylvie. Her concerned expression quickly lit up as she smiled once more. "My prince, you look so handsome. I regret my time with you is over," she said flirtatiously.

"Don't worry, Sylvie, I will not forget you. Not with all that mouth does." He gripped her chin in his large hand and raised her face.

"You do mean the jokes with which I entertain you?" She giggled.

He placed his other hand on top of her head.

"Good girl, Sylvie. Yes, you are funny. I will come see you for more jokes."

Sylvie looked genuinely pleased. I watched as her chest rose and her hand wandered longingly to his chest.

Desire is the true beast here, Leadanah commented. She gets wet just looking at him.

But she still looks afraid, I thought back.

The Prince is as evil as he is handsome. They say that about the devil, Leadanah mused.

Marston said, "I am sorry for Kandrah. Tell the girls, will you?"

"We will celebrate Kandrah's life, darling. May I send funds to her family?" she asked, still smiling.

"Yes, of course, whatever you think is appropriate. I will tell Annabelle to agree to whatever you request." He released her and stepped back. "Best you walk behind us now, Sylvie. Take your place. Annabelle will have a hard enough time adjusting without seeing you standing beside me, too."

"Of course, my lord. I will support her," she said with a polite courtesy.

Marston moved to the doorway and waited with his back to us.

"Silvie, why does Marston hate Rathon so much?"

"You don't know?" She seemed aghast.

I shook my head. She dropped her voice so Marston would not overhear.

"This is not the time to discuss it, but Prince Marston's eldest brother was killed in the rebellion." She paused, choosing her words carefully. "It is said that Rathon is the one who defeated him, but that it was not an honorable fight."

"Come, Andley, place your hand on my arm now. We must go into the castle together." Marston looked back at us and beckoned to me. "And smile. I don't like long faces."

I obeyed and stood by his side. I stared up at as he looked down at me. The sun was shining into his beautiful eyes, but they seemed to absorb the light and give none back.

This man will bring me nothing but suffering, I thought.

I placed my hand on his arm and smiled brightly.

"For your people," he taunted

"You have made it so," I said.

We walked together down the carriage's high staircase. Below, I could see an arrangement of nobles and royalty. The King stood before us with a woman who must be his high-mate; Marston's mother. The King was smiling up at us, but his mate held her face in quiet contempt. A look I would become familiar with in the following weeks and months. The Prince reached the base of the staircase and extended his hand to his father and bowed low. I stood stupidly next to him.

"Andley," he hissed. "Bow."

I started slightly and dropped into a low courtesy, my neck stiff. I could feel myself shifting slightly, and fine fur cropped up around my body.

"Alright, rise," the Queen hissed. "This is enough, my love. Let us go in."

Turning abruptly, she strode angrily into the palace. The King turned and followed his mate with a shrug.

"Come, Andley. Mother seems to hate you already. Wonderful!" he said jovially.

He flashed a winning smirk my way. One of his pointed teeth caught the light as he turned, tugging me along. He transformed into his dimidium, and his forearm grew and flexed with hard muscle as coarse hair sprung up from it. His already tall stature rose several inches. Suddenly, he loomed over me, blocking the sunlight.

"You're going to have one hell of an evening Andley. I wish Rathon were here to see." His words bit, and my stomach dropped when he grinned wickedly at me.

"Daddy!"

There was a harmony of joyous shrieks at the top of the staircase, and three small children scampered down, the smallest of whom resembled a black bear cub in his full therio form. He held onto the edge of each step and stepped down carefully, falling behind his siblings.

"My babies!" Marston shouted with equal and genuine joy.

He pulled his arm away from me, reaching for the first child, a little princess who looked to be around five with big green eyes and black hair. He scooped her up with his massive hands and held her to his face, plastering kisses all over her cheeks and forehead, while she held his face in her tiny hands, giggling. The other two children reached him and wrapped their arms about his legs, laughing. The cub released his father's leg and scampered up his back, holding onto his shoulders, nuzzling his father's neck. Marston ruffled his fur and leaned into him for more cuddles.

Leadanah watched intently from the back of my mind.

Remember this, Andley: no man is so evil that nothing can bring him hurt. That man loves his family.

I knew I should put a stop to such talk, but like a cold shadow insidiously creeping along a floor as the sun draws away, I felt myself leaning into Leadanah's darkness. Thinking of Kandrah's frail body, bruised and torn to ribbons only helped to expel thoughts of resisting it.

I followed the royal family up the staircase to the main entrance of the vast castle, watching my feet pass the stark barrier of the sunlit doorway into the awaiting darkness, where the stone no longer glittered. The cold settled into my skin, and my stomach lurched as the doors slammed shut behind me.

***

I could not eat. I found myself disgusted with every item displayed. Not just because of the strange practice of devouring infant creatures, or because of the heavy consistency of the sauces or the potency of the mead. I could not comprehend the decadence of it. I had attended feasts of course, but the excess of this was offensive, especially when I recollected the lean and sickly people we'd passed on the outskirts of the city.

The feast began with wild mushroom soup topped with creamy cheese and freshly baked rye bread. While at home, I very much enjoyed freshly made mushroom soup, but the aroma of sage and basil struck my senses like a punch in the nose. I bade the servant to take it away. He offered me a salad instead, but I found it to be smothered with a heavy, sickly sweet sauce.

I'd picked at it politely until the main courses were served. Before me lay plates of lamb smothered in fat, and piglets stuffed to the brink with baked figs and apples. The smell of their flesh weighed in the air, mingling with sweat and mead. The head table where I sat was laden with other types of meat I could not recognize, along with baked vegetables and exotic-looking fruit.

In the forest, we'd always had more than enough, even lately, although our people were growing leaner by the day. I looked around the great hall where every noble of the kingdom had been gathered for the mating feast. The roar of careless laughter and chatter was deafening within the great hall. There were however, two other morose faces.

The Queen was seated at a high table next to the King. Her beautiful face was drawn as she drank deeply from cup after cup of red wine. She stared bitterly at her food and seemed as uninterested in the food as I was.

A servant bowed before her, asking if she wanted something else from the kitchen. She picked her tray of food up and poured it out over his head. The food ran down his shirt in a river of soup and gravy. A clatter echoed across the hall as the dishes shattered on the stone floor.

The man rose from his bow with an air of polite servitude plastered firmly upon his face. "I will tell the servants the Queen is not hungry and to bring your wine."

He strode across the hall just as though hot soup was not running down his back and wetting his trousers. The King looked only mildly annoyed by the scene.

The other face was that of Annabelle, the Prince's old high-mate. Prior to the feast, there had been the oath-swearing ceremony. She'd been forced to stand before us all and declare her blessing of the new union. In turn, Prince Marston declared that she would have a place as his concubine and could remain with the children in their own quarters. She had stood stoically until that point, but her face flushed deeply in that moment as a look of relief and despair crossed her eyes in quick succession. Her hard eyes held Marston's gaze with an intensity that should have had the man begging for forgiveness. At the end of this, she'd leaned into him, and he kissed her cheek with the softness of a butterfly.

"You are still my love," I heard him whisper, as though this whole horrible ordeal was not his idea at all.

I watched as she closed her eyes in pain and returned his kiss. She stepped back with her hands clasped over her wrist, nails digging into the joint so hard the hand beneath was turning red. She and I accidentally made eye contact. I could feel her seething hatred for me radiating from her watering brown eyes. I wondered how, if they had love between them, could he have done this terrible thing to her? Was his hatred for Rathon and our independence so strong that he could tear apart his own life and family for it? Why?

Right now, she was sitting with the rest of the Prince's harem at the first table in front of us. She alone remained in her human form, and I wondered why, for she was very plain and slightly plump. But I had been informed that all the harems were required to hold their bodies in the exact forms Marston liked best. There seemed to be an order to the tables; that the harem came second to the Prince's table was only a little heartening. The lesser mates seemed to be part of the decor. They were all scantily clad in brightly colored gowns that exposed the parts of them Marston liked best. Some were in their full therio, while others were allowed to remain half-formed in dimidium.

They all seemed tense apart from Sylvie. She wore a deep blue sleeveless satin gown with a bodice split in two all the way to her pelvic bone. In the center, instead of bare breasts, there were bright pink feathers. They split tastefully to expose a small gap between her pert breasts. It was the first time I had seen her face in her therio form, but I doubted it was fully formed. Her lovely hair was replaced with more pink plumage, each feather faded to white at the tips. Her eyes were those of a bird, large and round but now the color of amber. Small soft feathers lined her temples and cheekbones, highlighting her features like makeup. Her nose had taken on a slightly sharp, downward turn. As I watched her, Marston saw my gaze and called a servant to us.

"Yes, my lord?"

"Tell Sylvie I will have fewer feathers upon her breast and more over her shoulders. She will know what I mean."

I looked at him startled, wondering how anyone could hold a form so specific. He looked at me with amusement.

"All of my concubines are expected to hold their forms to my liking. I expect you will figure it out soon enough." His eyes glittered, and he smiled wickedly. "Sylvie is best at it. You should follow her lead; it will make your life here easier. Look how happy she is. You could thrive here, Andley. It doesn't have to be a torment for you—just Rathon. As a matter of fact, the happier you are the better. Perhaps after a time you will forget all about that dog. Won't that be painful for him?" He finished with a laugh.

"My lord, why do you hate him so much.? To have done all of this, it seems, only to spite him," I asked.

"I do not like your talking," he said curtly. "Now watch."

He reached forward, turning my chin back toward Sylvie. The servant was whispering in her ear. She smiled pleasantly. I could see her mouth form the words thank you. She then looked at Marston and me, smiling. She offered a small wave and began shaking her shoulders furiously. The feathers on her chest fell to the floor. The dress only covered the outside of her breast, so her nipples were exposed to cool air. Still smiling, she raised a finger to her mouth and licked it playfully. She brought her wet finger to one breast and caressed her nipple, while new feathers shot out from her shoulders, cascading to her elbows. Some rose upwards, like a dragon's spikes along her shoulders. She gave the Prince a wink before going back to her pleasant chatter.

Annabelle looked at Marston, rolling her eyes angrily. Sylvie sensed her displeasure and reached for her hand, squeezing it. Annabelle looked back down at her plate and squeezed Sylvie's hand in return before releasing her and dropping it to her lap beneath the table. Marston watched this with mild interest.

"Why does Annabelle keep her human form? She is dressed so modestly?" I asked.

She was wearing a plain bronze gown with a collar that rose up her neck and covered her arms. Marston looked at me. The amusement flew from his face.

"I already told you to be silent. But so things are clear, you are my mate in title only. Lady Annabelle has my children. You think I would parade her like a whore for the rest of these pigs?"

"Why have you done this to her, then? For vengeance?"

"Why?" he spluttered, spitting his mead back into the goblet. "You do not know? Are you an idiot?"

"I must be. I have heard your brother was felled in battle and that Rathon ended him. But warriors die. Surely you understand the nature of war?"

The stinging in my face arrived so fast I hardly had time to realize he'd raised his hand at all. My face swung to the side and spit flew from my mouth. Raising a hand to my lip, I saw the spit was in fact blood. The room was momentarily startled into silence, but the chatter quickly rose back to a roar once again.

I raised a hand to my swelling lip.

"Never been struck before, have you?" He laughed.

I shook my head slowly, staring at him in bewilderment.

My hands trembled beneath the table, and I shivered as though I had been plunged into cold water. I glanced at Sylvie. She was staring back, her eyebrows knitted in momentary worry. Next to her, Annabelle was leaning forward with her elbow on the table, her chin resting on top of her hand. She had a slight, satisfied smirk on her face.

"Your rebellion split Sandor right down the middle. Cut the kingdom off from the valley. From our trade routes. Decimated our army. And your so-called king did not defeat my brother in battle." His voice seethed from between his sharp teeth. He gripped his goblet so tight it cracked. "He and his wolves slaughtered him like beasts. Warriors? Rathon and his pack are wild dogs with no honor."

"We sought freedom, not honor." The words burned my mouth as they slipped from my lips.

"Freedom? No. Power. Rathon's father sought power. And when he died, Rathon sought power." He leaned into me, whispering in a low growl. His lips brushed against my neck. For a moment, I feared he would tear me open.

At that moment, the Queen's voice rang through the hall. All were silent once again as they took in the scene.

"I cannot tolerate another moment of this. How dare you, oh mate of mine, allow this? Your own grandchildren's mother! Sitting there beside that gaggle of our son's whores. Would you seat me there with your own rabble as well? Why they are allowed in the great hall? I have never understood!"

Marston leaned over to me, seeming to forget what had just passed between us.

"Mother has never approved of allowing my harem into the hall. But Annabelle is more permissive; she almost insists on having my other mates around her. Mother never let Father's girls anywhere she could see them. Sometimes I wonder if they have not all simply died, forgotten in some abandoned wing of the castle. Father really gives her too much leeway." He leaned back in his chair. "But it is his kingdom. If he wants to be gentle with her, it is up to him. Personally, I would never tolerate such behavior, even from a queen. I admire him, though. As far as I am aware, he has never lost his temper with my mother. Even Annabell gets a swat if she's too mouthy," he finished, sounding slightly bored.

The King rose gracefully and held his hand out for his mate.

"Darling, come supper is finished. Let's turn in and let the youngsters have their fun." His voice was soft, but stern.

She crossed her arms and turned away.

The King held his hand out patiently. Slowly, she turned back to him and reluctantly clasped it in hers. He caressed her palm gently and led her out.

Marston watched them leave and snapped his fingers for a servant. "Inform Annabelle that the consummation will begin shortly. She may retire to join the children. Tell her I will join them in her quarters when I am done."

"And the rest of your harem my lord?"

"They will remain for the duration."

"Yes, my lord."

"My lord?" I began.

"Don't bother," he hissed. "I hope Rathon hears all about it."

"Have you done this to all of your mates?" I whispered.

"Just you."

He looked at me, smiling wide, all his sharp teeth exposed.

At that moment Annabelle, her face like a stone mask, rose and left without a backward glance.

Chapter 8
Andley

Leadanah lay asleep somewhere behind my mind, unaware of where we were. I resolved to leave her there no matter what the man did to me. He would have none of her. Not our body; not her scorn; not even her deadly wrath.

Marston rose from the table with his massive hand on the back of my neck and pulled me to my feet. I got up without resisting, determined not to make a mockery of myself and allow these people to watch me flounder while trying to fight someone several times my size. He held his hand there as we walked from the dining hall and turned down a long, narrow, candlelit hall. The progression of partygoers followed behind, whispering excitedly. Our steps clattered on the stone floor, but the tapestries lining the walls muffled the voices of the people behind us. Time slowed as we walked toward a door. It grew steadily as we approached until finally he bade me stop before its heavy wooden frame.

"Take off your slippers. We like to keep the carpet clean," he said casually.

"Carpet? I asked, staring up at him confused.

"The rug, Andley," he said in slight amusement.

I stared with my mouth slightly open, completely lost.

"Just take off your slippers," he barked.

The crowd behind us let out a soft giggle. Sylvie came up beside me, placing her arm on my elbow.

"It covers the floor, dear. Don't be alarmed by it. Here," she said sweetly. She knelt and gently lifted my foot and removed my slippers, placing them neatly beside the door. The floor was damp and cold. One of the servants moved to pull the door open as Marston also slid his shoes off, using his toe on each heel and kicking them aside. As the door pushed inward, there was a muffled scraping sound. I looked down and leaped back, alarmed. There was a strange bright blue substance covering the floor like a strange grass.

"No, Andley it's ok, it's just a carpet. It covers the floors so our feet don't get cold. I had never seen one before I came here either," said Sylvie.

Marston reached around my shoulder, making a shooing motion at Sylvie, who backed away quickly. He urged me forward, but I hesitated at the threshold, stumbling before the strange substrate as I tried to test it first with one toe. He pressed my shoulders forward, forcing me into the room. I pushed back against him, nearly falling in the process, afraid the wash of blue would be cold or sharp or that I would sink into it.

I had just took note of its plush softness when, with a swift scooping motion, he picked me up, cradling me in his massive arms. The crowd clapped lightly and giggled with pleasure, presumably; they thought the gesture to be romantic. Encompassing the round chamber wall were carpeted cascading rows of benches.

Oil lamps lit the room, casting a harsh dancing yellow firelight across the rounded walls. There were two rows of round tables set around a pit in the center of the room. Servants quickly pulled chairs out for the nobles and began pouring wine and lighting small candles to place on the center of the tables. Marston carried me past these as the crowd behind us seated themselves around the room on the benches and at the tables. An eerie quiet settled in the room.

I peered down the pit in the center as we approached. A massive round bed filled the hole. Sheer curtains covered the sides with the top remaining unobscured. From the top, anyone looking into the center of the room would have an unobstructed view of the bed below. It was down onto this platform that Marston carried me.

I looked up as he eased me down onto the soft sheets. He stood at the foot of the bed for a moment, drinking me down with his brown eyes.

He pulled the shirt from his waistband and slid it up his body, exposing a chiseled torso. The firelight flickered, casting dancing shadows across his body and the walls surrounding us. He dropped the shirt carelessly to the floor and reached for his belt, unbuckling it while locking eyes with me. My breath caught, and a spark flashed within me. Prince Marston was art— carved from clean marble. I could scarcely believe this was the figure of a living man.

With one hand, he drew his cock from his pants, massaging it in long, easy strokes. His forearm flexed as he stroked himself, drawing his cock up as it grew. He lowered his pants past his hips to kick them off his feet. He leaned forward onto the bed, coming for me with his half smile, reminding me again that he was a monster, thirsty for my pain. Goosebumps rose throughout my body, and my heartbeat quickened.

"You can have what you want, in private, please," I pleaded.

He ignored me and moved closer, creeping up toward my legs. Marston stopped, kneeling over me. He ran his free hand over my thigh, caressing my skin with soft ease, squeezing lightly, pressing his claws into my flesh.

"This can feel good, Andley. I can give you that. Just be a good girl and do what I say."

His voice was a low whispering rumble. My body betrayed me. A shiver crept up my spine while heat rose between my legs. I grew wet against my will as his light breath brushed through my hair. He rested a giant hand between my breasts, feeling my heat race.

"No," I gasped quietly.

"No?" he asked with a small smile.

"No." Tears slid down my cheeks.

"No, you won't do as I say? Or you don't want it to feel good?

"No."

I was an impostor within my body. He reached down between my legs, sliding a finger along the length of my vagina. He looked amused.

"Such treachery. Your body is not your own. What would Rathon think? I've barely even touched you."

He lifted his finger to his mouth, licking it.

"Were you and Rathon lovers? That's quite inappropriate, don't you think?"

I shook my head.

"What, Andley. Use your words."

"No," I whispered, helpless.

"Poor Rathon. Let's hope he hears about how I'm about to make you moan. I don't care if it's from pleasure or pain."

With that, his hand was suddenly on my throat, cupping my lower jaw. He turned my head to face him. He moved his legs in between mine, prying my knees apart with his muscular thigh. At the same time, he slid a finger—still wet with my own arousal—across my mouth, forcing my lips apart.

"Open your mouth, Andley."

I obeyed.

He slid his finger deep into my mouth, forcing my chin forward, while thrusting himself inside me. His girth forced my legs wider, and I snatched in a sharp breath, making a slight squeaking noise. His eyes locked onto my own.

"Pain?" he asked.

I turned my head away, but he forced my face toward him once more. He pulled back slowly until the head of his cock was in danger of slipping out then slammed its full terrible length back into me. He rammed two fingers into my mouth and down my throat, moving them in and out in time with his hips. I gagged and whimpered. His hand was still pressing down on my ribs between my breasts. I could barely draw in air between the weight of him and his fingers blocking my airway. Tears welled in my eyes as I became more desperate for air. I wrapped my hands around his forearm and tried to pull his hand away from my mouth. My hands didn't even fully make it around the circumference of his muscular arm. I knew how small I truly was.

Fear rocked me as his relentless thrusting into me pressed on, seeming to force me deeper into the bed with each stroke. Wretchedly, I could feel myself becoming wetter and wetter, feeling him slide along the walls of my vagina. God, make it stop, I thought.

"Does it hurt, Andley?" he asked, his voice husky.

Still pulling on his arm I nodded my head, frantically trying to breathe. "What?"

He pulled his finger from my throat finally.

"Yes."

I gasped, panting, trying to get my fill, afraid he would force his fingers back into me. Instead, he began rubbing my nipple his fingers coated with my saliva. I felt it harden under the rough caress.

"Doesn't seem to hurt," he mused. "You're very wet."

I covered my face and let out a disparaging moan.

"They all like it at first, Andley, but you surprise me. You should be ashamed of yourself."

His thrusts slowed, relieving me of the pain but leaving the wretched pleasure in its place. He leaned down, licking my nipple while still rubbing the other in small wet circles.

"I'm going to make sure you're properly shamed. It would be kinder of me just to hurt you and enrage Rathon. But I'm going to make you moan first. I'm gonna make sure you cum for me."

"Stop." I tried to push his mouth away from my breasts. "I don't want it."

"But you do." He laughed. "Oh, you fucking do. You're not as sweet as you want everyone to think."

I tried to ignore his short, shallow thrusts into me, his hands engulfing my breasts. His claws grazed lightly on my rib cage. My breaths became short hitches inward.

"Fuck, you look so pretty trying not to like this."

Marston slid one hand down between my thigh and rubbed his thumb slowly on my pulsating clit. He pulled his cock out and replaced it with his fingers. He hooked them forward, feeling my G-spot.

"Please," I moaned.

"Please what?"

"Stop." I gasped. "Please, stop."

"Ah, a fighter till the end."

I felt an orgasm begin to wash over me and tried pointlessly to move his hand away.

"You're too small, sweetheart. Why don't you try changing? Maybe your therio is strong enough."

He stopped rubbing my clit, holding his thumb lightly over it while he worked his fingers inside me, prolonging my shame.

"After you cum, I'm going to hurt you with my cock until you transform into your therio. Believe me, Andley, your human form is much too small to handle me. I hope you're ready to give me what I want."

His hand worked faster inside me. The walls of my vagina tightened around his fingers, and I resisted the horrible urge to rock my hips in time with him. A pleasurable moan escaped my lips like the beginning notes of a high song. I covered my mouth and turned away. He grabbed my chin once again and forced me to look at him.

"Look at me. I want to see your face when you cum. I wanna watch your eyes water and cheeks flush while you try to hide it. You can't hide your moans from these people."

His thumb glided gently around my clit again, and my moans intensified behind my hands. He replaced his cock inside me, and his girth drove me to finally cum. His eyes locked on mine.

"Don't you dare look away."

I stared up at him with seething hatred, wishing he wasn't so beautiful. This must be what it's like to get fucked by a devil. I felt hot tears slide down the side of my face, wetting my hair. I couldn't tell if they were there from the devastating pleasure or shame. In between my moans and gasps, I cried out my hatred, gasping out every curse word I knew. All the while the orgasm crashed through me with each thrust and pulsating contraction of my pussy on him. He bit my nipples, tugging and licking lightly, intensifying my pleasure.

"Fuck yes," he moaned. "Ahh fuck that sounds so hot," he said, referring to the undignified moans escaping my lips in between curses.

I could hear polite clapping from the spectators beyond and little gasps and ooohs of interest and arousal. I looked past Marston's wide shoulder and saw them at their tables and bleachers. They were pleasuring themselves and each other. I saw many men, cocks in hand, spurting off. Some of them had their hands buried in the bodice of the woman next to them. One man had a woman bent forward on the table before them, thrusting into her, both watching Marston and I intently. The sounds of their moans wafted into my ears as my own subsided.

I looked back at Marston's amused face.

"Gross, aren't they? Fucking animals. What do you think is more fucked up? That I would do this to you, or that not a single person here thinks it's wrong." His words came out in thin slices between his teeth as he continued his merciless thrusting.

He laughed in between his words, grunting lightly between thrusts. His cock was pressing even harder, filling me out more than before. I cried out; surprise mingled with pain as his next thrust felt deeper. His cock filled me as it throbbed, growing as he allowed his therio to break through. I couldn't help but let out more little sounds of pleasure, I'd never been so full before and didn't know how good it could feel with something this big inside me.

He slid back slowly, letting me feel every inch of him after each thrust. His cock was longer each time. The fur on his chest and stomach filled in more too, and his chest grew wider still. The muscles in his arms swelled beneath my fingers. His whole body engulfed me, all the while his cock growing in proportion. Soon my sounds of pleasure became sharp cries of pain.

"Oh, oh no, stop," I begged.

"No."

He kept up his steady pounding, growing a little more with each movement until half of his cock remained outside of me, unable to press in any further.

My screams grew louder as he slowly pressed himself deep into me, pushing on my cervix.

"Let's see your therio, Andley."

I began striking his biceps pitifully and pulled my hips into the bed trying to escape his cock.

"Transform, I want to see it!"

"No, no, take it out!" I cried.

He pulled himself out. I rolled into a ball, hoping it was over. Suddenly, he grabbed my hair, pulling my head back, forcing me to stare straight up at the ceiling. He bit down on my neck, piercing my skin with sharp canine teeth. A warm rush of blood soaked the pillow beneath me, staining my hair. He slid himself back into me, torturously slow, making me anticipate the horror of his depth. He stopped midway through and made short gyrations inside me, confusing my body and drawing out more sensations of pleasure.

"Stop, stop," I gasped.

He carried on, forcing my body to shudder beneath him, dragging another orgasm out of me. He thrust himself back into me, and my moan turned into another shriek of agony.

"Transform, you stupid bitch!"

His breaths grew shorter as guttural groans emanated from him. I slapped and punched his back and shoulders. I brought my knees up into his hips and tried to pry him out of me.

"My prince Marston," a shimmering voice trickled down to the bed.

"Huh?" he grunted, looking up.

It was Silvie, standing there beside the bed leaning in politely.

"My prince, I don't like to interrupt you," she said cheerfully.

"Fuck off, Silvie!" he roared.

Nervous, tittering laughter followed gasps from the crowd.

"My darling, I'm afraid you may kill her. I don't think that would be a good ending for your guests. Everyone is having such a wonderful time, and I'm sure you don't want to get carried away."

Marston sat up, getting to his knees causing his cock to draw back mercifully.

I turned my head to Sylvie, but he saw this and forced my face back toward the ceiling. With his free hand, he slapped Sylvie across her face, then drove his open palm in between her breasts and shoved her away. Turning back to me he slammed his cock fully inside me. His girth felt like it would tear me in two. He pulsed his hips into me once again, but was far gentler now. To my dismay, my vagina pulsed with pleasure.

"Oh, you like that huh?" he leaned in, whispering against my neck. "Guess I can't kill Rathon's little doll the same night I take it from him."

He bit my shoulder; the points of his teeth dug into the swollen wound he'd already given me. Soon he was snapping at my chest and breasts. Leaving small nip marks all over my body while driving himself into me, mercifully stopping before he could slide his whole length in.

His breathing became harsh as his rock-hard cock throbbed inside me.

"I'm almost done. I'll bet no one's ever gotten cum all over that pretty face of yours."

I let out a shameful little moan.

"You're going to look so good with it running from your face into your hair."

I scowled at him. Surely, he wouldn't.

Marston's thrusting became more hurried, his grunting more urgent. Then he slid himself out of me. I wrapped my arms around his neck, pulling my chest up into him while simultaneously wrapping my legs around his waist. I locked my ankles together around him as he tried to pull his cock out. My whole body went with it as he lifted back. I flexed my lower abs as hard as I could, driving my hips into him and forcing his cock back in, deep. It hurt, but I smiled as the look of bewilderment arose in his face.

"What the fuck do you think you're doing?" he growled.

His massive hand pressed down on my hip, but slipped on the sweat beading off my body. I thrust myself forward again and felt his cock pulsate inside me as he let out an involuntary moan. I thrust myself onto his cock several more times, feeling him spurt into me with each stroke. Holding my mouth close to his ear, I whispered, "Rathon is going to kill you someday."

I felt my pussy clench as the image of Rathon ripping this monster apart with his bare teeth and claws fluttered through my mind. I imagined Marston's blood spilling out of him as he lay beneath Rathon's rage. Finally, Marston slammed my body back onto the bed and tore his cock out of me.

"I'll fucking kill you!" he growled, wrapping his massive hand around my throat.

I imagined his blood still spurting from him as he rose over me. His pulsating cum spilled into my open, laughing mouth. It ran out of the corners and down my cheeks. As he had predicted, it spilled over, pooling around my hair. As his cock drained, he grabbed hold of it and moved downwards so the rest poured down onto my tits, flowing down the center of my chest onto my stomach, beneath my breasts, spilling over the sides of my ribs. I watched his penis pulsating and throbbing in his hands, horrified and fascinated.

He leaned forward, intent on his promise to shame me, and pressed my breasts together while sliding his cock in between them, spreading the warm fluid around. He held one massive hand over my breasts, squeezing them together, his claws digging deep into my flesh. His free hand kept a steady pressure around my throat, pressing harder and harder. I looked up into his face. His eyes were excited as he watched the life being squeezed out of me.

"My lord you mustn't!"

I heard Sylvie's voice like a bell beside me. There was an uproar in the background.

"You will start a war if you kill her!"

For the first time since I had met her, Silvie's voice rang with genuine fear and anger.

Everything went black.

www.ingramcontent.com/pod-product-compliance
Lightning Source LLC
Chambersburg PA
CBHW030553130626
46552CB00006B/2527